Curse of the Boyfriend Sweater

Patricia and Adam Scribner

CURSE OF THE BOYFRIEND SWEATER

.

PATRICIA AND ADAM SCRIBNER

CURSE OF THE BOYFRIEND SWEATER

Dedication

To our family at Patricia's Yarns, we love you.

CURSE OF THE BOYFRIEND SWEATER

Preface

"Ask any knitter, and she will tell you: it is bad luck
to knit a sweater for your boyfriend."
- The Daily Knitter

CURSE OF THE BOYFRIEND SWEATER

Chapter 1: The Girl in the Boyfriend Sweater

It happened in seconds.

In New York City everything moves so quickly.
Seldom does time slow down enough that you're
able to recognize the carefully worked seed stitch on
a hand-knit, dark blue, Merino wool sweater;
especially on a girl blazing past you at rush hour
speed.

But I saw it. It was *my sweater*.

I had spent months transforming ten balls of extra-
fine Merino wool into a stunning gift for my
boyfriend. He obviously never cared how much time
I spent picking up stitches and making sure each knit
and purl were perfect. Obviously, he never cared
how I tailored the sweater just for him, taking
clandestine measurements when he wasn't looking
or was dozing beside me. I spent all of my spare time
on this beautiful sweater, sneaking in hours when
Dennis wasn't home in order to make sure it was a
surprise.

Why was *she* wearing the sweater that I knitted for
him?

If I had taken the subway one more stop, I may
never have gotten off in front of the Layton Imperial
Hotel. But it was the first nice winter day in weeks,
so walking seemed like a great idea. Snow was

turning into an oozy mess at the curbside, the morning New York sun blazed brilliantly as it came up above the buildings, and even – big surprise for a January day – I heard birds chirping! They were tricked out of their winter slumber by this gorgeous day. Tricked, just like me.

Dennis was supposed to be in Seattle on business. Dennis – Mr. Cool, Calm, and Collected –looked me in the eyes and said, "Jane, I'll be home by Friday night. It's just a quick trip to the West Coast for business." God! And I believed him! I believed almost everything he said; after all, why shouldn't I? He was the handsome advertising executive who had not only asked *me* to move in with him, but also provided a home and all the Tribeca amenities a 25-year-old girl could ask for during the past three years.

Yet, there *she* was, with her tousled hair and slight grin. She looked tired, and happy, and – god dammit! – *cozy* in the sweater. Her evening dress draped down her slender legs from underneath the sweater. She was stunning, even when wearing a knit sweater and an evening dress, and she walked by so confidently and self-assured.

He spent the night with her. And he gave her *my* sweater to wear home in the morning. How many times had Dennis lied? Was this the first time? Did our history together mean nothing?

CURSE OF THE BOYFRIEND SWEATER

Was there ever really a history to mean anything in the first place?

I wanted to yell at her, but I found I couldn't move. After she walked past, my eyes were stuck to the pavement. Morning commuters jostled past me, some elbowing me aside, – *"Watch out! Jeez!"* – but I barely noticed. I couldn't believe it. I couldn't breathe. I felt cold, cold and alone, cold and mocked by the tricky January sun. *Go away sun!*

All those hours I had poured into making that sweater for him. He didn't care.

I blinked back the tears that formed in my eyes. *I will never knit a Boyfriend Sweater again!*

***

"Jane, I'll be home by Friday night. It's just a quick trip to the West Coast for business."

Dennis and I stood in the kitchen as I put some of the dishes in the dishwasher. He held my shoulders, his arms out straight, and looked me straight in the eye. His Dennis look. His *I'm selling you something* look. And I bought it.

He let go of me. "I'm leaving tomorrow afternoon right after work."

"Give me a call when you get in?" I asked.

"Sure. Although I've got a meeting as soon as I land."

"OK, well, just call me sometime tomorrow night. Maybe when you're in transit?"

His eyes were elsewhere, looking around the kitchen; gleaming, shining. And then he suddenly turned to me: "Did I tell you about the ad I wrote?"

"Which one?"

"The thing for Sir Hugs-a-Lot diapers? Oh man, Janie, it's so great. The mom's got the little kid in her arms, right? And then all of a sudden, the Jaws music goes on like, duh duh, duh duh, duh duh. And it's a slow-mo zoom-in on the kid's face, like, 'oh crap, here it comes, *what is happening*?' And then it cuts to the mom, and she's really happy, right, like she's holding her baby and everything, but then her face totally changes, like, 'oh NO, I know what's coming, I know what happens when that music comes on,' and he has the Other Diaper on. Then it cuts to another kid held by his dad. This kids wearing *Hugs-a-Lot*, but when the Jaws music gets ready to go, nothing really happens and the dad is still smiling and the diaper is fresh and clean-looking. That's the point. Get it? With Hugs-a-Lot, you can still really love and hug your kid even when they're crapping it up in your arms."

"Sounds pretty funny."

"Oh my god, you have no idea. Ken and Abe ate it up. I pitched it to them and they were like, 'Denny, *write it. Write it now.*' "

"Babe, don't worry about the dishes, just get Yolanda to do them tomorrow."

"You mean Maria?"

"Yeah, yeah. Yolanda." Dennis strapped his iPod to his bicep in one of those elastic iPod sleeves.

"It's ok," I said. "I like doing it."

"You're so *domestic*." He clicked the button on his iPod and started some warm-up in-place jogs. Cymbal clashes and muffled synthesizers bled out of his earphones.

"No," I said. "I don't mind doing dishes. It is only a couple more cups anyway."

"OK, I'm going out for my run. See you later?" he said loudly, over the sounds of his headphones.

"Yeah – wait, Dennis, I want to give you something."

"Oh yeah?" he shouted over his music. "Can it wait till I get back? Got to get my run in, can't do it in the morning. I have to plug in early at work, since I'm catching a flight."

"Well, I can give it to you when you get back from running"

"Sounds great. See ya soon! Oh, don't delete Entourage on the DVR."

"I wasn't going to."

"No, no. Just the one from last night – I want to make sure I see it." He kissed me on the cheek and left, running out the door.

***

There I was, standing in the middle of a busy sidewalk, one strap of my shoulder bag on, one strap off, falling slowly to my elbow. I worked up the courage to call Dennis.

"Hi Jane," he said to me when he picked up the phone. He was so calm. *How could he be so calm?*

"I… I… I saw her," I stammered out.

"Who?"

"You gave her my sweater!" I yelled.

"I didn't give anybody your sweater. Jane…" he said, his voice suddenly groggy. "It's like 6 a.m. here. Why are you calling so early?"

CURSE OF THE BOYFRIEND SWEATER

Oh, Dennis, you can't fake it!

"Dennis, I *saw* it - on a girl walking past me. I would know that sweater anywhere."

"That bitch stole my sweater?"

"You mean you didn't give it to her?" My heart was lurching – maybe I had been wrong about the whole thing. Maybe he really was in Seattle.

"No, I didn't give it to her. She must have taken it out of my suitcase."

"Who?" I was panicking. "Dennis, how do you know her?"

"*Look*, Jane," he said, sighing, "I could lie about this. I could say she stole my suitcase at LaGuardia and here I am in Seattle, sweater-less and suitcase-less. Though I guess that would be a bit of a stretch. But I'm going to take the proverbial *moral high ground* here, and let fly with some reality. That babe, who you saw the sweater on…"

"What, Dennis?"

"She's my boss's sister. She drove Ken to the airport and we met there. She didn't have a sweater, so I loaned her the one you made."

"Wait, really?"

"No! God, Jane, it's just that I can't stand *lying* to you. It's so hard. I just want to be a good man."

"Then what was she doing with the sweater? Tell me the truth, Dennis."

"The truth."

My stomach turned. "Dennis, I think I can figure it out."

"Jane. Listen, Jane. Let's not make this a Big Deal."

"*A BIG DEAL?* You cheated on me, Dennis!"

"Janie, I am really requiring you to attain a level of chill right now. I'm being the big man here. I'm fessing up, coming clean. The least you could do is reward my honesty with some gratitude."

I looked up. The street signs read 25th and 6th. Somehow I had walked 10 blocks past my office.

"Dennis, are you even in Seattle?"

"Mmm…no.

"Where are you?"

He sighed. "I'm at the office."

I could hear the faint clicking of a keyboard in the background.

"Jane," he sighed. "I'm going to be serious for a minute. We've been together a long time, and I think that we're moving in two different directions. Oh – hold on a minute, Jane." I heard him cover the phone with his hand and muffled noise in the background. "Jane. Are you there? What I was saying: I don't think it's meant to last between us. I need to start seeing other people."

"What?"

"You should get your things and move out of my apartment."

What? How long has he been thinking about this? A thousand questions flashed through my brain at once. But I couldn't even comprehend what he was saying.

Dennis worked in advertising. His words were his tools. His advertisements were funny and clever. They were supposed to make people feel good about buying the products he promoted.

He could also use words to be incredibly hurtful.

I was staring straight ahead, staring at nothing. A great calm descended over me. I hung up the phone.

***

I went through work like a zombie. I didn't talk to anyone but my clients. Despite the reasonable salary I was earning as a physical therapist, all of my loans from NYU made it feel like I was barely scraping by. It had helped that Dennis took care of the rent and most of my living expenses.

What was I going to do?

Too overcome to deal with patients any longer, I signed out of the office early. The warm winter day was turning into another cold January evening. As soon as that tricky sun went down (*at 4pm! Who ever thought Daylight Saving Time was a good idea?*), the old winter chill came back. But this time, I didn't have any home to go back to. No perfectly furnished Tribeca loft, no down quilt to snuggle under, no aromatic tea collection, no late-night dessert wine in the perfect crystal snifter, no big-screen TV with my favorite shows Tivo-ed up and ready to watch, one after the other.

I shivered as I walked around the Tribeca neighborhood where I had lived for the past three years. The neighborhood Dennis and I had walked together. It seemed to betray me now. All of the places I knew, the places we were together, seemed to laugh at me. I felt foolish.

CURSE OF THE BOYFRIEND SWEATER

How could he do this to me? When you're a little girl and you envision a knight sweeping you off your feet, you never expect the knight to have another princess. Or two. Or three. Or – oh, who knows? I didn't know what to do. I was upset and scared of being alone. And I couldn't sleep in Dennis's apartment – God, no! What was I going to do? Where would I stay?

I fumbled through my oversized Coach bag, full of yarn and needles, and reached, once again, for my phone. I called Rachel.

"Hello Janiee!" Her voice came alive. She was always so bright and cheery.

"Rachel…" I could barely get out her name. My tears were in full stream now.

Her tone changed in an instant. "Oh God, what happened? Are you ok? What's wrong?"

I started to explain and she told me to meet her at her apartment. She said she would leave work immediately.

There was a restaurant on the ground floor of her Chelsea building. I saw people inside laughing, ordering desserts, and standing in groups at the bar. Even though I was cold and a little sweaty from the countless blocks I had walked to get there, I waited outside. I didn't want to wait inside with a bunch of people who could care less what had happened to me. I stood under the awning – looking down, trying not to make eye contact with either the doorman or the residents returning home from work.

"Oh Jane, I'm so sorry," Rachel said. I lifted my head to see her. Her arms wrapped around me. "You're shivering. What are you doing out here in the cold? Let's get inside."

Rachel was my best friend. Even though I was taller, our mannerisms, our looks, our behaviors were so much alike that we were often confused for sisters. We joked about having different mothers, but the same father. It was amazing to us how many people bought it. In 9th grade we actually had our geometry teacher confused for a good two months, and were able to fake absences and exchange homework pretty easily. Of course, it wasn't pretty when the teacher found out what we had been doing.

Rachel and I grew up together in a small town in North Jersey. We had learned how to knit side-by-side over winter break during the fourth grade. We made a pact in the sixth grade that when we grew up we would both have fabulous jobs and a fabulous apartment in the city. It was our plan.

Rachel always had plans. She planned for us both to go to NYU. She planned for us to live in New York. She planned to get a job in fashion. Now, she worked as a stylist in the Fashion District for a large fashion house. Her plans always seemed to work out. I needed her to help revise my plan.

She took out a burgundy red and a couple of glasses from her cabinet. "Glass of wine?" she asked. I was sure this was a good first step to any plan.

Sitting side by side on her couch in her cozy apartment, we discussed my need to take time off from work and how to get my things out of Dennis's apartment.

My life with Dennis had not been perfect. Living with him was sometimes lonely. As an advertising executive, Dennis usually worked late into the night to meet clients and often left on business trips.

Business trips – what a joke! I wondered again how many times something like this had happened. He "left town" at least once a month, sometimes two weekends in a row, and sometimes four times in a month.

When he was home, we rarely talked. He was 32 and I was 25. I didn't think the age gap mattered too much. After all, plenty of girls my age dated older guys, especially in the city. Yet I knew there was something wrong with the relationship, but it was hard for me to tell anyone. After all, I was young and living in a trendy loft in Tribeca with a dishwasher and a maid. A *maid*. My life *seemed* perfect.

"How could he do this to me?" I said again, burying my head in Rachel's lap. I knew there was no response that would make me feel better.
"I don't know," Rachel said, stroking my hair.
The hardest thing would be explaining it all to my parents and friends. Rachel told me it didn't matter.

"Jane, I'm here for you. I feel like we haven't seen each other in a long time. I'm always working, you're always out…"

"I know," I sniffled. "I'm sorry."

"Don't be silly. But you know I'm here for you."

"I don't know what's going to happen. What should I do next?"

She reached across me to take the bottle and my glass off the table. "How about you call out sick tomorrow and drink another glass of red?"

I did not refuse.

Chapter 2: Old Friends

Light came white through my blinds, not gray-blue like it had the previous several mornings. Christmas day and white light like that meant only one thing – snow! I jumped out of bed, kind of amazed that I had slept that long on a Christmas morning. (The year before I had jumped on my parents' bed at 5a.m. and they faked reluctance to go downstairs at that hour to open presents.) I opened the blinds. Sure enough, snow was swirling everywhere before me as I gazed down onto our backyard. The yard was a sheet of white, trees were folded in frost, and the picnic table was lost in a mound of drifting snow.

I slipped on my bunny-eared slippers and bounded into my parents' room, but they were already downstairs.

"Morning, sweetie," my mom greeted, sipping hazelnut and cinnamon-flavored coffee as I slid into the living room.

"Morning Mom! Merry Christmas!" I looked around, but it was just Mom sitting there, a pattern for green-and-blue stitch mittens across her lap. "Where's Dad?"

"He went out to get some scones for us."

Scones and coffee on Christmas Day was a family tradition. There was one bake shop in town that was open on Christmas morning, and they made a killing selling scones on Christmas Day. Usually, Dad would have been back by now, but I figured he had a late start.

"Oh, ok," I replied.

My mom smiled, "but it gives us a little time together right now. I was hoping you'd get up soon!"

"Here sweetie, before Dad gets home, I want to give you this special present from me. " She took out a lumpy package from next to her on the couch, and handed it to me.

Inside the wrapping was a beautiful ball of dark gray wool and two large wooden needles.

 "Wow, thanks Mom."

"I think it's about time you started your own projects. I bought this gray yarn to match those stormy eyes of yours." She added, "Rachel's mother said she was going to get Rachel a beginner's set too. Since you'll see her later today, I thought I might help you both learn to knit!"

Rachel's family was Jewish, but that never hindered our getting together on Christmas Day. In fact, it was something of a tradition for her to come over on Christmas (and for me to give her a present and her to give me one) and Easter: and, for me to go over to their house during Chanukah and Passover. They weren't exactly the strictest Jewish family (and let's face it, we weren't the strictest Catholic one – I think we averaged four masses a year), but it was nice to be able to share in a little multi-culturalism, especially with my best friend; and particularly in the North Jersey town where we grew up that celebrated its cultural diversity.

Rachel came over later in the morning and we exhausted ourselves playing in the snow and sledding in the park near our house. Just as the sky was beginning to turn orange and purple and grey and the little Christmas lights started twinkling on around the neighborhood, my mom first taught us how to cast on.

For our first project, my mom decided to teach us both how to knit – what else? – a scarf. It was a little tricky at first, but Rachel and I got the hang of it pretty quickly. Our moms had picked out chunky yarns in our favorite colors: gray for me, and navy blue for Rachel. The scarf called for five knits per row, and we used big size 17 needles – easier to hold with our small hands.

Luscious steaming mugs of hot cocoa with little marshmallows melting away inside sat on the table beside us. While Rachel's mug of cocoa was downed pretty soon, I was so absorbed by the knitting that when I looked over to my cup, the marshmallows were soggy and the hot chocolate cold. I looked up at my mom as I was beginning my tenth or so row. She looked so proud as she watched Rachel and me.

SIMPLE SCARF

Yarn: Rowan Big Wool
Needles: Size 17

Cast on 5
Knit every row.
Knit until two yards remain.
Bind off loosely.
Weave in ends.

I finished that scarf in two days, all over Christmas break, and it wasn't long before my mom began showing me patterns for hats and mittens.

***

I woke up the next morning on Rachel's couch. The night before, after I had fallen asleep, Rachel placed a large glass of water on the coffee table next to me. I drank every drop. My eyes were still sore from tears.

It was Thursday. Fortunately, as Rachel suggested, I had called my physical therapy office the night before. It was a small office. One could only call out in emergencies. Rachel and I both agreed this counted as an emergency.

Rachel woke me just before leaving for work, tapping me gently on the shoulder. "Shhh. Don't get up," she said.

Rachel looked great. She was wearing her signature pair of jeans and heels, and a V-neck shirt under a long black trench coat. She always had a way of looking so stylish and comfortable at the same time.

I ran my fingers across the dark blue blanket covering me and remembered the nights I sat up making it. It was stitched in four patterns: a chevron stitch, a basket weave, a garter stitch, and a seed stitch. I knitted it in Rachel's favorite color, dark blue. I had wanted to give her the blanket the day she moved into her apartment. In my usual fashion, however, I gave it to her three weeks too late. Later, she would tell me she stayed under it for days after her boyfriend broke up with her. Life is full of cruel irony.

When I got up, I checked my phone for messages. A text from Rachel read, "Stay as long as you want. XOXO."

Even though I had been in Rachel's apartment a million times, I had never been there alone. Walking around, it was easy to recognize her impeccable taste. Her bedroom had large walk-in closets filled with designer clothing only talked about on red carpets. Her bed was a beautiful four-poster and her bathroom was Italian marble. Her kitchen had chef-grade appliances and clean stainless steel surfaces. Whitewashed antique furniture softened the hard modern tones of her loft. I secretly wished her place were mine. I envisioned my new life as a single girl beginning there, but I knew I could never afford it. It was after noon before I finally made my way back into the winter cold. I wore the clothes I had been wearing the day before. I walked back to Tribeca to get a bag of my things. *What if Dennis is there? He should be at work.*

I paced back and forth in front of the building maybe four times. *Oh, this is stupid,* I thought. *I should just go in. Screw him if he's there or not!*

With my head down I walked past the doorman, into the building, and onto the elevator. I stepped out on our floor. My hands shook as I fumbled to use my keys in the door.

"Hello, Jane." I jumped. I turned. It was Lori, my next-door neighbor. She was returning with her daughter asleep in a stroller. "How are you?"

"Fine," I said. I bit my lip to remain quiet. My stomach fluttered.

I opened the door to my old life.

The apartment looked the same. Maria had already been there that day. As usual, nothing was out of place. I stared at the bed. It was already made. Clean and crisp, the sheets pulled taught, nine extra-soft downy pillows arranged neatly in stacks over the upturned edge of the comforter. *Did that girl sleep there with him?*

I remembered the first time I brought my parents to the apartment three years before. They were so impressed. I was living in a New York City apartment the same size as their modest suburban house. The apartment felt more like a museum than a home. Mies Van der Rohe chairs and large Basquiat paintings displayed the wealth Dennis had amassed at a young age. Even his Ivy League friends were impressed.

"Robert De Niro lives in the same building," he bragged to my mom and dad. "I saw him the other day in the gym upstairs. Guy's pretty buff."

The apartment was very Dennis. Very little of it was me.

Picking out my belongings, I wanted to leave quickly. I couldn't get my things fast enough. I only needed to get essentials: first thing I grabbed were my knitting needles. Then I took my knitting bag with two skeins of unwrapped wool packed inside. I stuffed my large handbag with cosmetics, a few pairs of jeans, a sweatshirt, a sweater, and my jewelry box. I left the necklace Dennis had bought two weeks before on the bedside table.

Rachel had already helped me plan for movers to come later that weekend to get the rest of my things. I hailed a cab as soon as I left and took a deep breath. *Did I lock the door?* It didn't matter. I gave the cab driver Rachel's address.

Rachel came home early from work. When she asked me if Thai food and more red wine would help make me feel better, I didn't hesitate, "yes." I realized I hadn't eaten all day. We spooned at a pint of Ben and Jerry's before dinner was delivered.

"I never liked him," Rachel confided. "I always felt that Dennis was looking for the next best thing, Jane."

"Really?" I asked. "Why didn't you ever tell me that before?"

"I don't know."

Chapter 3: Silver Cufflinks

"So, what do you do?"

I was talking with this guy in a bar in the West Village. It was about 10 or 11 at night, springtime of my senior year. Graduation was right around the corner. The place was loud. People crushed to the bar, sweaty arms clamoring to get the bartender's attention. "I'm a student. At NYU."

"Oh, yeah . Of course you are." He slugged his tonic down. Sweat matted the hair on his forehead. His tie was loose and hanging down from the collar, and exposed a hairless upper chest.

"Um." Pause. "I'm about to graduate."

"Oh, man. Wow. Sorry for you. Suck the marrow out of your last bones of freedom. Free bird." All around me the music blared, and, in a typical NYC meat-market scene, sweaty guys in suits and oxfords hit on girls two-thirds their age. I was here with a couple of friends from school, celebrating the end of college; they were scattered to the winds.

"So, where do you work?" I asked him.

"Well, as soon as I graduated from The Big D I got a job here at old Barnesy and Ross. So, you know. Living the dream. Advertising. NYC. Hot women. Whatever."

"Hot women, huh?"

"You wouldn't believe. No, just kidding. Sorry. I'm a little buzzed. What did you say your name was again?"

"I didn't."

"That's a weird name. Eyedint. Is that like, Scottish?"

"No, it's Jane."

"Ha. Yeah. Jane. You're funny, Jane. Plain Jane. Not that you're plain. You're pretty hot. That's a nice name, Jane."

"Thank you."

"That's also a very nice sweater."

"Oh," I said and looked down at my sweater. It was my favorite gray cotton cardigan, perfect for cool spring nights. "Thank you. I knitted this myself."

"No *way*! You, like, *knit*?"

"Yeah."

"That's *crazy*. I didn't know chicks still did that."

"Well…some do."

"So, Jane the NYU Girl, what are you, like, *majoring* in? Knitting? Grandmothering skills?"

"Physical therapy, actually."

"Actually? Oh, cause you thought I thought you majored in, like, something else? Post-feminist ideology or something."

"No…I actually was a history major, but then switched over."

"His-story! You wanna know *my* story? Ha… Sorry, bad joke."

"That's ok."

Just then he turned around. Somebody had grabbed him by the shoulder.

"Is this big hunk of man-flesh bothering you?" A stranger stepped in, well-dressed, well-groomed, shining white teeth. Dressed kind of like the other guy, but better. Nicer. Nicer fitting suit.

"Denny! What is up? Jane, have you met my primary pal, Dennis, over here?"

I was a little short of breath. Dennis looked at me, flashing this big smile. "Yeah, he is bothering me, a little bit, actually," I said finally.

Their eyes widened. "Oh Jane is very feisty," the stranger said.

"Hello Jane, I'm Dennis. Pleased to meet you." He extended his hand. His perfectly tailored shirt pinched back just a tad as his hand reached out to take mine. As I put my hand in his, time slowed down, sparks were flying. And a classic silver cufflink was visible on his French cuff.

"Hello, Dennis. Nice to meet you, too."

Chapter 4: Breaking Up

By Friday I still hadn't spoken to either of my parents about the break-up. I especially dreaded sharing the news with my mom, since she had never been supportive of my moving in with Dennis in the first place. She thought I was too young to be living with a man, much less an older man.

So when she called me first thing on Friday morning, I resolved that I would try to let the revelation slide another day or two, just to see how I was handling things.

Yeah, except she could tell from my voice the second I picked up the phone.

"What's wrong?" she asked immediately.

"Nothing," I said. "I'm alright."

"Jane?"

I took a deep breath and told her the whole story: the sweater rushing past me, the call to Dennis, Seattle and the lies, and the nights I had been sleeping at Rachel's.

"Are you at work?"

"No," I said. "I took the day off."

"Good for you. You need to rest. Why don't you come home today? We can take care of you here."

"No, mom, I'm fine. I'm at Rachel's."

"Jane, you can't stay there forever," she said. "You're welcome to move back home," she added quickly.

I knew she would ask me to move home. I also knew that moving back home would only make me feel worse.

"Your father and I miss you so much. We have so little to talk about these days. We would love to have you move back in with us," she persuaded.

"Mom, I miss you too," I said, "but I think I need to figure things out for myself. I've been talking to Rachel about getting my own place. I've never had one."

"Can you afford the city on your salary?" My mother always had a way of bringing me back down. "Dennis was the one making all the money and you still have loans from NYU. Why don't you move home for a while until you get your feet under you?"

"Mom!"

"I'm sorry sweetie," she said. "I know you're going to be fine." Her comments didn't reassure me. "What are you knitting nowadays anyway? I'm working on a baby blanket for your cousin's new baby."

"I'm not knitting right now," I fibbed. "Let me call you later."

I didn't want to talk anymore. I didn't want to talk about Dennis or where I would live. I didn't even want to talk about knitting. By the time I hung up the phone, I was more disheartened than ever.

"You can stay on my couch as long as you need," Rachel later said with a hug. "I'll help you box-up your things at Dennis's place this weekend."

***

Saturday, with Dennis away, Rachel and I went to get the rest of my belongings. In a matter of minutes Rachel arranged for the movers to come later in the evening, take the boxes, and put them in storage.

Rachel had a type-A personality – a major requirement for a job like hers. She was a stylist – a job that required her to think fast and get things done. I was with her one year at Fashion Week in the city and her phone didn't stop ringing. With fabric in one hand and a cell phone in the other, she directed the daily schedules of 20 different runway models. I was frantic just watching her.

What Rachel wasn't good at, however, was sorting through my personal items. "Throw this away?" she asked, holding up a shirt I had bought only two weeks before.

"No!" I said. "I just bought that!"

"Ugh." She threw it in the "Tentative" pile. Rachel was high fashion. She wanted me to be high fashion, but I was not. On most days, she wore designer clothes. I wore Levis, t-shirts, and sweaters that I knitted myself. Except, of course, when Dennis told me what he wanted me to wear.

We put the last of my framed pictures in a box and stacked the boxes near the door. We were ready to leave when I walked over to Dennis's wine fridge, with his stupid Cornell magnet on it.

"A Bordeaux from 1995," I said to Rachel, and pulled the bottle from the fridge. "He bought this for us the day I moved in." I took the prized wine and placed it in my purse. "Screw him!"

"Nice," Rachel said with a smile. "Let's have it tonight." She grabbed my hand and we left.

Rachel and I were walking arm in arm two blocks from my old apartment. "I'm going to take you to your favorite restaurant," she said with a smile.

"Amilda's?"

CURSE OF THE BOYFRIEND SWEATER

Amilda's – a tiny hole in the wall restaurant in SOHO (like really tiny; I read several online reviews where people said they actually walked right past it several times, it was so hard to find) where my parents would take me when they visited me in college. They had delicious desserts (my favorite was a French-style pear galette with almonds and caramel and vanilla gelato). More importantly, I had never had dinner there with Dennis ("The Menace," as Rachel now called him).

We sat at their bar sipping cosmopolitans and eating chickpea fritters - on her tab, she insisted. Up to this point, Rachel had avoided asking me questions about the breakup.

She licked a finger. "When did you know he was cheating?"

"Not until I recognized the sweater I knitted on that woman when I was going to work," I replied. "And then he told me on the phone. He's such an ass."

"I'm sorry Jane. We don't have to talk about this."

"No, it's ok," I said, shaking my head. "It's the Curse of the Boyfriend Sweater."

"Oh my god, you're right," she said.

"I know. I put the sweater in his suitcase before he left because I wasn't sure he liked it when I first gave it to him. He came back from his jog, and I was like, 'here, honey! He sort of held it up and looked at it and was like, 'oh yeah, wow, thanks'."

"That's all he said?"

"That's it. I *still* can't believe he gave it to *her* to wear. It's crazy." I shook my head.

"I'm sorry Jane," she repeated. "I know it's hard to believe now, but you're going to be better off. Dennis is a jerk."

"I know, I know. I just don't know what to do next."

"You don't *have* to do anything."

"Rachel, where am I going to live? I can't afford the city," I said shrugging my shoulders.

Rachel, like my mother, offered to let me stay with her. Unlike my mother, however, I knew she didn't want me there forever.

"You'll love having your own place," she said. "I do."

"I've been checking every neighborhood in Manhattan on craigslist , but I can't really find anything I like or can afford."

"You should move to my neighborhood!"

"Yeah right. Like I can afford that now."

"I'm sure you could find a cute place somewhere downtown."

"Not according to my search. Not unless I hit the lottery."

"Well, what about uptown? I hear there are a lot of big places up there. Look in the Upper West – you could just take the 2 or 3 subway to work. Or, what about somewhere in Brooklyn?"

"No boroughs. I'll be too far from work."

"Ha, no boroughs." Rachel laughed. "Well, you could always move back to *New Jersey*. Have your parents as roomies."

She was grinning , but I was thinking. "New Jersey…?"

"What, you think I'm serious?"

Rachel looked surprised.

"Oh my god," she said, "You're not going to move back in with your parents? Jane, no."

"No, no! I'm not going back there. But, New Jersey – what about Hoboken? Maybe Jersey City?"

"Hoboken?" She stuck a fritter in a little ramekin of horseradish sauce. "I guess it would be ok. I've heard Hoboken is…nice," she shrugged.

"Rachel, this could be perfect. My physical therapy office is on 14th Street. Hoboken would be such an easy commute – easier than Brooklyn for sure, easier than the Upper West Side. Hey, can I borrow your Blackberry?"

"Sure," she said, eyeing me suspiciously. She wiped her hand on a napkin and dug around in her purse.

I Googled *yarn shop + Hoboken*. "There!" I said, "Google says Hoboken has a knitting shop!"

"Are you serious? Only you would decide where to live based on knitting!"

"Will you come check it out with me? It's called Patricia's Yarns."

"You can't leave Manhattan, Jane."

"I have to," I said. "I certainly can't afford the neighborhood you live in and I want a short commute. Plus, I think Hoboken could be really cute." I grabbed a fritter and took a bite. "Will you at least come with me to check it out? If we hate it, I won't move there. But it's at least worth a trip back across the river."

Rachel looked crestfallen. "When do you want to go?"

"Tomorrow?"

"You'll have to take the PATH," she said, like it would change my mind.

"It's just another subway line to me."

"I guess we're going back to Jersey." She lifted her glass.

"Back to Jersey!" I raised my glass to meet hers. "Cheers!"

"I can't believe it," said Rachel, tipping her martini glass and finishing her drink.

Rachel had spent her life planning how to get us out of New Jersey. Now I was thinking about moving back. I often think back to the days we were in high school, driving around town bored out of our minds. New York City was only twelve miles away, but for some reason we never went that far, the divide too large to overcome.

That night, after returning from dinner, we sat on her couch in pajamas and started knitting. I began a pair of mittens. Although she was a good knitter and could do everything a good knitter could, Rachel hated following patterns. She decided to start another scarf.

The stash yarn I took from my bag was handspun and hand-dyed, its colors arrayed in a beautiful rainbow pattern. It's called *Wildflowers* by Manos del Uruguay. I love the feel of the yarn and watching the colors unravel and blend, stitch by stitch, into a beautiful multi-toned palette.

We sat for hours, knitting, laughing, and drinking Dennis's Bordeaux. I was feeling better again. By the time I drained the last drop from my glass, I had already bound off the thumb of my first mitten. One down, one to go!

JANE'S MITTENS

Jane's Mittens

The mittens are knit in the round on double-pointed needles. You begin with the cuff, working on the smaller needle, and knit in a rib pattern for two inches. Then you switch to stockinette stitch and to the larger needle and work the hand of the mitten while increasing for the thumb gusset. Put the thumb stitches on a holder, cast on over the gap, and continue knitting the hand of the mitten to the end of your pinky. Decrease for the hand and finish off. Pick up the thumb stitches, knit, decrease and finish off.

Please note there is a list of abbreviations at the end of the book.

PATTERN
Yarn: Manos del Uruguay Wool Classica, 2 skeins.
Guage : 18ts = 4 inches in st. st. on lg. needle
Sizes: Adult small, (med., lg.)
Finished hand circum.: 7" (8", 9")
Needles: US 6 & 8 double pointed needles (dpn's)
Notions: stitch markers, scrap yarn or stitch holder, yarn needle.

CUFF
With #6 needle, CO 32 (36, 40)

Divide Stitches on 3 double pointed needles:
Needle #1: 12 (12, 14), Needle #2: 10 (12, 14)
Needle #3: 10 (12, 12). Join in rnd being careful not to twist stitches. Work K2, P2 rib for 2 ½" (2 ¾", 3")

HAND
Change to st. st. and larger needle (#8) and work ½", about 4 rounds.

Set-up thumb gusset: on needle 1, for all sizes, knit across 2 stitches, place marker M1, K1, M1, place marker.

1. Knit 3 rnd even

2. Increase rnd, knit to marker, M1, knit to marker M1, slip marker, knit to end of rnd.

3. Repeat above 4 rnds until there are 11 (13, 15) gusset sts between marker.

4. Knit to 1st gusset marker, remove marker, put sts on length of yarn as holder. Remove 2nd marker. Knit to end of round and increase 1 st. at base of thumb to 32 (36, 40) sts.

5. Work even in st st until hand measures approx. 1 ½" (1 ¾", 2) or to tip of pinky.

TIP OF MITTEN SHAPING

Dec. as follows: K6 (7, 8) K2 tog. Repeat around.
Knit 1 round.
Cont. working 1 decrease rnd with 1 less st (ie. K5 [6, 7], K4 [5, 6] k2tog) followed by 1 knit rnd until 8 (9, 10) sts remain.
Cut yarn leaving tail and pull through.

THUMB

Pick up sts off yarn and divide evenly on dpn's.
Pick up and knit 1 st. from base of thumb @ gap – join in rnd   12 (14, 16) sts. Work in St st. for 1 ¾" (2", 2 ½") or try on as you go – should end at tip of thumb.
Shape top

K2 tog around 6 (7, 8) sts rem.

K1 rnd

K2 tog around until 0 (1, 0) sts. Remain.

Cut yarn and pull through.

Weave in ends, use yarn to close hole at base of thumb & enjoy!

Chapter 5: Back to Jersey

It was freezing cold on Sunday when we stepped off the PATH train. Hoboken is a riverfront city, and the wind whipping off the Hudson reminded us it was definitely January. The cold found its way to every spot of bare skin. We closed our coats, folded our arms, and walked like New Yorkers to warm up.

From my first steps across the cobblestone streets I could tell Hoboken was charming. Peeking East down the city's side streets, we could see magnificent views of New York City. The docks along the Hudson seemed to float on the slate-gray water, and skyscrapers darted in and out of swirling clouds of mist. Oak and cherry trees, looking unclothed and shivering in the cold, stood in rows along the streets. Above, new, sleek condominiums towered over stately, squat brownstones.

Despite the cold, mothers were out pushing children with strollers in one hand and hot coffee in the other. Loud cheers came from the numerous Irish pubs on First Street, even this early on a Sunday. Fashionable dresses hung off mannequins in quaint shops' windows, and crowds of people crammed onto restaurants' porches stomped their feet and blew their hands against the chilly morning as they waited for a brunch table to open up.

"Wow, it's cuter than I remember. I would live here – if it wasn't in New Jersey," quipped Rachel.

CURSE OF THE BOYFRIEND SWEATER

We made our way into a coffee shop and began to map things out. The barista handed us our coffees and pointed to a free local paper. He told us we could find rental ads there. It was good to be in from the cold. We sat down and started sipping our lattes. Rachel was keyed into craigslist on her Blackberry while I scanned the listings in the paper. "The prices here are definitely better than in Manhattan. Here's a one-bedroom I can probably afford," I said, folding out the paper on the table so Rachel could see it. "In fact, I could *easily* afford it if I stop buying $4 coffees," I joked, taking another sip of frothy latte.

"You could easily afford it if you bought less yarn," Rachel responded.

"Let's be serious," I laughed. "I won't give up yarn."

"Would you give up buying red wine?" she asked.

"I might give up buying red wine," I said. "After all, I still have the keys to get into Dennis's wine fridge!"

After gathering some information, Rachel called a few realtors and lined up several apartments to see. Joe DiVincenzo, a realtor, met us at the coffee shop. Despite the cold, he was sweating profusely when he took off his ski hat. His hair was matted against his forehead, and little beads of sweat were defrosting on his temples. He extended his ungloved palm to us.

"You're lucky you caught me! I was supposed to show an apartment to another guy, but he cancelled on me at the last minute. I was in the neighborhood anyway. Ready to see some apartments?" he asked, smiling.

"Yes," I said, unaware that that was the last time I would sit until the end of the day.

"Freakin' cold out there," he said. "You girls got coats?" He asked Rachel, "You got a hat? If you need to borrow one, I have an extra."

"No, I've got one," she said, putting on the floppy black hat I had helped her knit about four years ago while we were still in college. "But thanks…"

As we crossed a street, Joe said, "You know, you've picked a good time to go looking. *Nobody*, and I mean *nobody*, wants to move into this city in January. With snow piling up on the sidewalks, it is impossible to get a moving truck in. Movers block the whole street off, with the snow at the curb and everything. Horns honking. Neighbors yelling. Garbage just sitting out there without the collection. It's a nightmare. Last year some guy's moving truck slipped on some ice coming out of the tunnel and fell in the Hudson. Everything ruined. Plus, pipes are always freezing this time of year. No hot water. Heating pipes bursting. Rats and roaches rather be inside than out, if you catch my drift. Jesus, it's a disaster."

I looked over at Rachel. She was staring right back at me, both of us wide-eyed.

"No, no," he continued. "No, but you girls are smart. Prices are way low. Landlords are looking for renters. Wanna fill up the apartments so they don't go another four months without a tenant. Nah, don't worry about it. Forget about it. There are no roaches or rats in Hoboken." He grinned at us.

Joe gave us a guided tour of Hoboken. We saw a studio apartment uptown (too drafty), a one-bedroom downtown (too decrepit), a high-rise by the waterfront (too pricey), and finally, Joe showed us a small one-bedroom with a tiny balcony situated right on Church Square Park.

The building had a bronze plaque on the front with "1902" emblazoned on it. The apartment was a third-floor walk-up. Its large windows and balcony faced the park and flooded the room with light. A public library was right next door. A lovely church whose evening bells had just begun to toll sat at the western edge of the park. The windows looked down onto a playground. Like many apartments of its era, the apartment had high ceilings and crown moldings.

I loved it.

Joe told me I could take immediate occupancy. He said I could move in the next day if I wanted. "No, no. Nah, great building. Great landlord. I know her myself. Lovely. A little deaf, a little bats, you know? But a nice lady. She'll cook you dinner probably when you move in. Move right in. Tomorrow. No, seriously. Great deal."

I was nervous about how quickly things were happening, but I was also very excited.

"It's really cute," encouraged Rachel.

We went back to his office and started filling out paperwork. I didn't expect to sign a lease that quickly, but I needed a place to live. I skimmed the lease (typical stuff – no pets, liable for damage, etc.) and took out my checkbook. I held the pen over the lease, and looked up at Rachel. She was smiling. I signed my first, middle, and last names to the words "oh. my. god."

"I can't believe this," I said.

"You're a Jersey girl again," said Rachel.

"I've always been a Jersey girl," I replied.

Afterwards, I encouraged Rachel to make one more stop: to Patricia's Yarns. Unfortunately, by the time we got there, a woman with a small dog was locking the doors.

"Are you closing?" I asked.

"Yes," she said. "Do you need something quick? I can stay open."

"No, that's ok," I responded. Although I was disappointed, Rachel seemed pleased the woman was closing up, as it had been a long day already. We were both really tired.

"I just signed a lease on an apartment here in Hoboken and I'm really happy to know there's a knit shop nearby," I told the woman.

"Welcome to the neighborhood! I'm Patricia."

When you think of a typical yarn shop owner, you think of a little old lady knitting in a rocking chair; someone in the Elizabeth Zimmerman mode; tea water bristling on the kettle, grandma giving you a gingerbread cookie, and cats purring in her lap. Patricia wasn't like that. She was young, probably in her late 20's, and pretty. She was tall, and was dressed in a fashionable skirt and coat that accentuated her tall frame. She spoke in a voice that was gentle, but confident. For the cold evening, she wore a matching hat and scarf that were so beautiful I imagined she knitted them herself. Her dog, Riley, a very cute Yorkshire terrier, was about the length of her forearm.

"I'm Jane," I said.

"Hi Jane."

"And this is my best friend Rachel."

"Very nice to meet you both," Patricia said.

From the outside, Patricia's shop was lovely and inviting. I looked through the Victorian picture window, with the Patricia's Yarns logo scrawled along the glass, at all of the yummy colors of wool, alpaca, and cotton. In the window, a cute child's dress hung next to a mannequin wearing a thick and wispy hand-knit mohair sweater.

"Where are you moving from?" Patricia asked.

"Not far—Tribeca," I said.

"Wow, your New York friends are going to let you move to New Jersey?" Patricia joked.

"I tried to keep her in Manhattan," laughed Rachel.

"Where in town are you moving to?" asked Patricia.

"Right around the corner, just across the park."

"Well, Hoboken's a good little city," responded Patricia, smiling. "I think you'll like it."

"Thanks," I said.

"Best of luck. I hope to see you again," said Patricia.

"I'm sure you will," I replied.

"Great! Stay warm!" Patricia, Riley trotting in tow, walked off down Fourth Street.

By the time we got back to Rachel's, we were both exhausted. I was so excited about my new apartment, however, that I somehow I found the energy to finish knitting my mittens.

I moved to Hoboken the next day.

Chapter 6: Hoboken

My new apartment was…different. Dennis's building was new and modern. My building was built over 100 years ago. I traded modern for, shall we say, quaint. Dennis had a stainless steel kitchen with concrete countertops and floors. I now had old-fashioned wood countertops – if you could call them countertops; it was more like a shelf in a tiny nook next to the old chamber stove, a stove which seemed to shake even when turned off – and parquet floors that needed shims for bookshelves and tables. The moldings in my new apartment had been painted so many times that they almost weren't visible. Instead of Dennis's large marble Saarinen dining room table, I would now eat on the floor until my couch and TV tables arrived from Pottery Barn. Instead of a king-size bed, a new double was on its way from Sleepy's.

I had also traded functional for falling apart. The first night, I tried to take a hot shower to warm up after a freezing day. I turned one of the little silver knobs jutting from the shower tile, and whoops! it slipped off. It clanged onto the shower floor and the loud clang nearly made me jump out of my skin. I picked it up and tried sticking it back onto the hook, but it wouldn't go on. Oh boy. I was getting a little frustrated: standing there in a bath towel that was slowly falling off, bent over my dysfunctional shower trying to shove the H knob back in place. I tried the Cold. Sure enough, it worked. But what was I going to do in a cold shower? I turned the shower off, left the broken knob on the sink, slunk into bed, and resolved to call the landlord the next morning.

I called out of work *again* to get moved in, unpack, and sort boxes. Although the movers got tired of me saying "the box says fragile," I was able to get most of my things put in the rooms where they belonged pretty quickly. It wasn't too hard—my new apartment only had one room and one closet; and frankly, my things could've been moved by anyone with a few hours and a station wagon.

After the movers hoisted the last box up the three flights, set it down, and closed the door behind them, I collapsed onto my bed. OK, next item on the list: call the landlord about the *shower*. Ugh. I was feeling gross and sweaty. After all, I hadn't showered since two nights ago at Rachel's. I scrounged around in my drawer and came up with the number Joe had written for me. I dialed and after a few rings, a little woman's voice on the other end said, "Yes?"

"Hi, Mrs. Genovese?"

"Yes, speaking."

"Hi, this is Jane Sullivan, the new tenant on the third floor."

"Who is this?"

"This is Jane. I just signed the lease for the—"

"I'm sorry, you must have the wrong number. Good-bye!"

Click. Dial tone. Hmm. Erg. I called back. Ring. Ring. Ring. I waited for I guess two minutes. I think that's a little too long for a phone to be ringing. She must not have an answering machine. A little unusual for a landlord. *What does she do when her tenants are trying to reach her?* As far as I knew, she was the super too. Joe didn't mention anything about anyone else; he said if you have any problems, give Mrs. G a call.

I tried one more time. Still no answer. This was really frustrating. I knew she was home. I knew she must hear the ringing. I mean, Joe said she was a little deaf, but *come on*, she had picked up the first time. Was she avoiding me? Oh my god – the realization dawned on me: was this a doomed apartment? Did she and Joe have a scheme to sell me on a decrepit old room that was falling apart? Of *course* no one wanted to move in during the winter. Suddenly my fantasy of a perfect pre-war one-bedroom apartment was crashing down like WWII London buildings during the blitz. *What other problems was I going to face?* I remembered Joe's litany of disasters plaguing Hoboken's winter apartments. Suddenly the pipes started clicking and clacking, rattling like they were about to burst. I felt very, very cold: there was a draft coming in through the window near my bed. I thought I heard a scratching under my bed: I jumped. A mouse? A rat? A big, glowering, slavering, red-eyed New Jersey sewer rat? Or worse: a family of rodents, a menagerie of crawling creatures, big and small, ravenous and ready to feast on every spare crumb I let slip from my granola bar? I imagined them scuttling in and out of the tiniest nooks in my apartment, crawling under my hand-knit alpaca blanket and brushing against me in the middle of the night. I saw flecks in my floorboards move. Yes? No. Just flecks. Not roaches. Not belly-up carapaced critters.

I felt like Macauley Caulkin's character in the first *Home Alone* when he goes down into the basement and imagines the furnace is a red-bellied hellish fire-breathing monster. Suddenly my apartment seemed like a horror-house.

I called Joe. Message machine. "Hiya, this is Joe, leave a message. I'll be sure to get back to you soon. J-E-T-S, Jets, Jets, Jets!"

D-A-M-N, Dammit. Dammit. Dammit.

I thought about going and knocking on the old bird's door on the first floor. Knocking till I knocked the door down. Huffing and puffing like the big bad wolf – but feeling like a poor little piggy up here in my cold room with no hot water.

I couldn't do that. I didn't want to impose.

I left a message. "Joe, I tried calling Mrs. Genovese but she hung up on me. Now she won't answer her phone. I know she's home. I need to get my shower fixed. I have no hot water, and the knob fell off, and it's *really cold*. What should I do? Call me back. Sorry, this is Jane. Sullivan. I just signed the lease on the Church Square Park apartment. Call me back. Thanks. Bye."

I hung up. Immediately my phone buzzed. Joe?!

No. My mother. I had forgotten she was coming over to help me put my things on shelves and set up the apartment. I tried to pull it together. I didn't want her to see me like this – she would say, "You should have come back to live with us."

I flipped open my phone. "Hi Mom."

"Sweetie there's *nowhere to park*."

"I know, Mom. You just have to circle around until you find something."

"I've been circling for ten minutes. I almost was rammed onto the sidewalk a minute ago by a maniac. This city is madness."

"Check near the hospital. There's usually a spot or two open there." Then the thought occurred: "Actually, Mom – why don't you just go down to the parking garage on Fourth and park there – I'll head out now and meet you."

"Is that near you? I thought I was going to come up and help you arrange your new apartment?"

"There's this great little knitting shop on Fourth I want to show you. I've been unpacking all day. I need a break. Plus, you would love this place. OK?"

"O.k. See you in a minute."

I got off my bed (checking the ground for varmints: none). I kicked the remaining boxes in a closet and shut the door on them. I grabbed my knitting bag, bundled into my winter coat, snatched my phone off the bed, and headed out to meet my mom.

***

When we got to the shop, we were greeted by a pretty blonde-haired girl sitting at a large, round table. "Hi! Patricia ran to get coffee. She'll be right back if you have any questions."

"Do you work here?" I asked.

"No…" she laughed. "I spilled my coffee and was in the middle of a row." She gestured to the coffee stain on her jeans. "Trish ran to the coffee shop for me. It's a half a block away. My name is Michelle."

"Hello."

My mom said, "Has anyone ever told you that you look exactly like Samantha from Bewitched?"

Michelle stared at my mom. "What's Bewitched?"

"Oh my goodness, you really date me. And I feel like that show just came on yesterday. What are you making?" my mom asked her.

"A lace shawl."

"That's beautiful," I said.

"It's really simple," Michelle said. "It's just stockinette and a few a yarn-overs."

"The colors are stunning," replied my mother.

Patricia, walking Riley with one hand and balancing a tray of coffee in the other, shouldered the door open in a burst of sleigh-bells and entered the shop. She greeted me. "Hello again!"

"Hi Patricia!" I said.

"Are you all moved in?" she asked. *She remembered me.* The smell of coffee from the cups nestled in the tray she was holding filled the room.

"Getting there," I said. "Patricia, this is my mother, Ellen. Mom, this is Patricia."

CURSE OF THE BOYFRIEND SWEATER

"Please let me know if I can help you with anything," said Patricia placing Riley on a chair and walking behind the counter.

"Thank you," replied my mother.

The shop had two full walls of yarn. Both sides had floor-to-ceiling whitewashed wooden shelves chock-full of cubbies packed to the brim with luxurious natural fibers. The high ceilings and polished hardwood floors accentuated the light from the huge front Victorian window. Dust-flecked winter sun also streamed in from a large window in the back of the shop. Nat King Cole played on the stereo. I knew I loved this place as soon as I saw the beautiful knits in the window, but the jazz on the stereo sealed it. "Sweet Lorraine, Lorraine…" I love jazz, and have a soft spot for any oldies recordings. The round wooden table and winged-back antique chairs set up around it invited people to sit and knit.

In the back of the shop, there was a bulletin board with numerous Polaroid pictures tacked to it. Each picture showed a person smiling and holding hand-knitted items. The hand-written captions said things like "Michelle's Fibre Co. Scarf" or "Mia's First Baby Sweater".

I have this thing when I'm in a clothes shop – maybe it's the knitting girl in me. I always go more for texture than look. I go around to every shirt, skirt, and sweater – and touch everything. I'll only try it on if I like the way it feels. That's why a knitting store is like a shopping paradise – so many textures to feel, so many soft yarns, different gauges, some fine and smooth, some thick and soft, that you want to sink into them.

I touched my way from yarn to yarn: cashmere, alpaca, Merino wool, organic cotton. My fingers and eyes stopped at a wool yarn in an off-white color. It was a blend of Merino and Mohair in a single ply, chunky weight. For a chunky yarn, it was not too thick, but also not too thin. I could tell that if I made a hat out of this yarn, it would be lovely and warm.

"I love this," I said, holding the yarn up.

"I use that yarn all the time!" replied Patricia. "What are you thinking of making with it?"

"I'd love to make a hat with this."

"I have the perfect pattern." Patricia opened a large black binder she pulled from the shelf and began flipping through the single-page patterns. "I just wrote this hat pattern for a friend using that yarn."

She opened the binder rings and took out the pattern of a winter hat finished in a berry stitch. The photograph attached to the pattern showed a model wearing the hat. It was the type of hat you would see on any Hollywood starlet: almost a beret, but loose-fitting, slouchy, and hip. With the white yarn I had picked, the hat would go with any outfit. It was exactly what I was looking for. Patricia handed me the pattern.

"Have a seat," Patricia said, and pulled out a chair at the table next to Michelle. She gave me a ball of the white wool.

"Thanks," I said. I sat down, pulled Size $10^{1/2}$ circular needles from my bag, and cast on. I knew the hat would be perfect for Rachel – it would go well with her fashion sensibility and would keep her warm. I decided to make it a surprise gift for her.

Though I was eager to start a new project with the yarn I picked out, my mother wasn't as easy to persuade. "I have such a large stash already at home…" she complained.

Eventually, though, she pulled two skeins of hand-dyed wool from a cubby. "I love these colors," she said, holding up the pastel-colored wool to her cheek, unable to resist.

My mother sat down next to me. Jazz played on the stereo, moving from Nat to big band to some cool bop. The brim on the hat didn't take long to stitch. When I finished it, it was time for the berry stitch pattern. The berry stitch has a great texture – bumpy and knotty, but still organized and carefully arranged. It proved a bit challenging in the beginning; but once I got moving I could see the hat forming before my eyes. When I began decreasing, slowly shedding stitches from my circulars, I switched to double-pointed needles, as the crown was getting smaller quickly. It was amazing how the berry stitch maintained its pattern even while decreasing. While I knitted, I asked Patricia about living in Hoboken. She offered her favorite shops and restaurants.

"Anthony David's is the best brunch place – you have to try it. You also need to try the chocolate store that just opened up next door."

My mom said, "Oh, yes, I saw that walking over."

"It's amazing. They have the best dark chocolate."

"With all the local shops, it's like a micro-economy right here," I said. "You guys come here to knit, get your coffee from the shop around the corner, and then you get chocolate for dessert."

"And when we're done knitting we go to one of the bars," said Patricia.

"Knitting, coffee, chocolate, and wine, do you need anything else?" Michelle asked with a smile.

"Right. I noticed a lot of bars in town. Where do you guys go on weekends?" I asked.

CURSE OF THE BOYFRIEND SWEATER

"You should check out L and J's – it's right up the street on Washington – and O'Nieal's – which is right on the park, so near you," said Michelle.

"Jane, you should come with us sometime after knit night," Patricia said.

"Knit night?" asked my mother.

"Every Friday I host a knit night at the shop," continued Patricia. "Some of us get together and knit and bring wine and snacks."

"You would love them," said Michelle. "You'll fit right in."

That comment made me feel great.

"What a great way for you to meet new people, Jane," smiled my mother.

When my mother and I left, I was nearly finished with the hat. The winter sun was long down. We walked the few blocks back to my new apartment by streetlight, orange and yellow, our shadows stretching and snapping, collapsing behind us. She had her arm in mine; my hands were mittened and shoved deep in my pockets. We huddled together as we walked along the frozen Hoboken streets. "I've never seen you take that long to buy yarn before, Mom."

"What do you mean? I *eventually* bought some yarn," she retorted.

"I know, but it took longer than usual," I teased.

"Well, money is tighter these days than it has been lately. I'm just being more cautious."

What? I wasn't expecting that response.

Her teeth chattered as she spoke. She drew in a long, sharp breath. "Jane, your father and I aren't doing so well."

What? I couldn't believe what I was hearing. *You tell me this now – after the week I had!* I looked at my mother and saw her wipe a tear from her eye with her leather glove.

"Oh, Mom, I'm sorry," I said. "What's going on?"

"No, I'm sorry. I shouldn't be telling you this now. You've been through a lot with Dennis and moving. And, we've had a nice afternoon."

My parents were the one constant in my life. I loved them both very much. Growing up, I never saw my parents fight. They might have ignored one another from time to time, but they never fought. Maybe I saw a few cracks – but never fault lines in their relationship. In fact, until that day, to me, my parents always seemed content.

"Your dad just seems very distant lately," said my mother as we approached the garage.

Hasn't he always been distant? This is the man who, on his 50th birthday, after we had planned a huge surprise party with about 50 family members and friends, was disappointed because he wanted to play golf from sunup to sundown; the man whose idea of a holiday is reading in a chair with the door closed; the man who went to bed at 9:30 every night after watching "Great Battles of the American Revolution." I love my dad a lot, but he's not exactly Mr. Social.

"Mom, it's going to be ok." I was unsure if I was telling her or asking her. I couldn't believe that I was now repeating to my mom what Rachel had told me only days before.

And I was so tired.

"I love you Mom," I said when we reached the garage.

"I love you too, honey," she said, hugging me.

"Drive safely."

As I was going up the first flight of stairs to my new apartment, I checked my phone. The voicemail icon was blinking – two new messages – and a missed call from Joe! I must have missed it while we were walking back from the shop. I had almost forgotten about Joe and the hot water crisis. I picked up the message. I stopped dead on the landing.

"Jane, hi, Joe DiVincenzo. Sorry I missed you before. Look, I called Mrs. G. She's aware of the problem. Sorry, I don't know if I told you before, but she's a little, uh, hard of hearing. She doesn't always hear the phone. Her doorbell is a super high-pitched doorbell that she installed two years ago after one tenant's dog bit another tenant's dog – really horrible, actually. One of the tenants tried to contact Mrs. G. for like three days, but she just sat in her house and couldn't hear anything. So, finally when they got through, I said to her, Mrs. G., maybe you need like a hearing aid? She wouldn't do it, but she did install a special doorbell. It's like a foghorn I swear. You can hear it on the docks. Boats get tricked by it it's so loud. Ha. I think once they caused a boat pileup on the river cause they all got confused—"

The message cut off. I listened to the next voicemail.

"Jane, sorry, Joe DiVincenzo again. I think I got cut off. So anyway, what I was saying: you should go down and introduce yourself to Mrs. G. She'll probably have you over for dinner. But I'm so sorry about that with the shower thing. It should be all fixed up soon."

Joe was about the nicest real estate broker in the history of the world. All of my old college friends, after graduating were kicked out of their NYU apartments. They told horror stories of NYC brokers as they searched for their first post-college apartments. How NYC brokers were a deviant and evil group of misers and cheats. But Joe seemed like the best guy ever.

Since it wasn't too late, I decided to stop in and see Mrs. Genovese. I rang her bell like Joe had suggested (and it was very loud!). I waited a few moments, and then I heard the same voice I had heard on the phone that morning. "Who is it?"

"It's Jane, the new tenant on the third floor," I said loudly.

I heard a bolt slide from its lock shaft, the click of a second lock being twisted out of the catch, a rattle as a chain was taken off a hook, a creak of the handle, and then the door opened.

In the doorframe stood the tiniest lady I think I had ever seen. I'm pretty tall, I think, in terms of height – 5'9" about. But this lady seemed like she was at least a foot and a half shorter than me. She was cute, and wrinkled, and so skinny that she seemed like she was made of almost nothing at all. Her hair was done up in curls (no curlers in her hair, just a curly dye-blond). She was wearing a tiny striped top that hung off her bony frame.

But what caught me even more than the sight of Mrs. G. were the smells coming out of that apartment. As soon as the door opened, I was hit by the most delicious odor of garlic and tomato and cheese and herbs and bread – like walking down Mulberry St. or some corner of the Village at dusk, when all the restaurants try to entice you in by your nose, and the smell on every street corner makes your mouth water.

"My gosh, that smells good! What are you cooking?" My question came abruptly before an introduction. I caught myself. But Mrs. G. was already responding.

"Oh, you like it, huh? It's just my Bolognese. Joe told me you would be coming by. He called me earlier today." She spoke with a slight accent; maybe Italian but also kind of New York.

"Yes, sorry, but my shower is a little broken. The handle…"

"Yes, yes, of course. I already had it taken care of."

"You did? When?"

"This afternoon. You weren't home. But I have a spare key."

"Thank you, Mrs. Genovese."

"It's nothing, it's nothing. You should have called me earlier, when it happened."

Could I have told her that I did…? Apparently she didn't remember. "You're right, I should have."

"Don't feel shy around me," Mrs. G. admonished. "I have nothing to do all day but sit around. I'm here to take care of my building and my tenants."

"Well, thank you very much."

"Can I help you with anything else?"

Her tone was a little short. I wasn't sure if I was disturbing her. The something else would have been that pasta. I was super hungry. Joe said that she would be very welcoming, and that I would probably be invited in for something to eat. But I decided not to mention it. "Nope, that's all. Good night!"

"Good night." She quickly shut the door behind her and started her locking ritual. I went upstairs and made myself a little toast. As the bread was warming in the toaster, I went into the bathroom. Sure enough, the hot knob had been replaced. I tested it. Presto. The bath water ran out of the faucet into the tub. I had to wait about two minutes, but soon steam started rising up out of the faucet. I turned the shower knob, and delightful, steamy, hot water poured out of the showerhead and fogged up my mirror. Mist started beading and whirling throughout the bathroom. I forgot all about my toast and jumped in the shower. Eyes shut, I stood in the warm water until my fingers pruned.

Toweling off, I saw my phone light blinking once again. I flipped it open: new text from Rachel: "Hope you love Jersey! Miss you! :P"

I hit some sort of emotional crux. I saw my knitting things there, needles akimbo and banded at the ends. A string of wool slowly pooling and winding back into a huge wound ball. One strand connected to a giant network of like color, like wool, intertwining. It's like me connected back to fellow knitters: at the shop, New Jersey, Rachel, my parents. It was too much. I felt tears coming up. But not tears about Dennis this time. Not tears of sadness. *Something else.* I was alone. I was, for all intents and purposes, *lonely*. My parents were fighting. Rachel was across the Hudson. I knew next to no one in this new city. I was like an island floating in my little window. One tiny lit-up window in a network of thousands of windows facing millions upon millions of tiny lighted windows across the river. I was connected to my old city – Manhattan – where I lived for seven years straight, first with roommates NYU assigned me, then with those I found myself, and then with Dennis for three years. Never paying my own rent – it was *Dennis's apartment* – connected to my old city only by a system of tunnels and railways and ferries. Terra non-firma. Water breached the gap, divided me in this new place from my old place. But this place was mine. Here I was, for the first time, at 25: my own apartment. My own furniture: my own bed that I bought; my own refrigerator with my own groceries; my own shower all to myself; and, while I'd be happy to share it all with someone else, someday, it all belongs to me.

I pitched over the side of my new bed. I covered my face with both hands, and tears leaked out down my cheeks. My body shook with something between joy and sorrow, but I felt some kind of deep connectedness to this new apartment and this new place.

Feeling exhausted and warm, thanks to the shower, I turned down the covers, rolled onto my side, tucked my pillow under my right ear, and fell fast asleep.

Chapter 7: Marvin

I dreamed that night about my parents. The dream recalled a scene from when I was a little girl, but it was weird and distorted in my memory. We were all having dinner out at some restaurant, but instead of talking with us, my mom was knitting. We were waiting for our appetizers, and my dad was talking to me, but I was just watching my mom knit. He took out a book and started reading. In the dream the book was called – I very distinctly saw the title – *Great Civil War Battles of the American South*. My mom kept knitting, not turning to my dad or me. We waited for the waiters for what seemed like an eternity. There was a Comfrey plant on the table. Finally, when the waiters came and put our food down before us, it started getting very cold in the restaurant, and snow was leaking through the ceiling. I couldn't see my dad anymore with the snow building up, and everything was turning white. Soon snow and wind were blocking my mom from sight…

I woke up to: "Another snow storm headed our way."

I had a small clock radio that rested on a box next to my bed. I sat up, remembering my dream in little nebulous wisps. The meteorologist on the radio continued, "we have already had record snow totals this winter and it looks like that trend will persist."

CURSE OF THE BOYFRIEND SWEATER

Morning broke through the dusty windows, cold winter morning light peeking through the white sky. The wool blanket I had knitted lying on top of my sheets felt too heavy to move. The tip of my nose nipped just a bit, that foreboding nip that makes you not want to get up into the cold. I knew I would have a freezing walk to the PATH train. I also knew I had to get back to work. I had taken too many days off from work already.

I hadn't slept too well. It felt like I was in and out of dreams and sleep all night. I distinctly remember waking up and seeing a blinking light from some window or roof across from mine through a space between my curtain and windowpane. I thought at first they were signaling to me in Morse Code. Flash, out. Flash, flash, out. Residents (or maybe aliens?) welcoming the new neighbor. But then I realized the window was slightly opened and it was just the wind blowing the curtain in front of someone's bedroom light . The dream of my parents seemed as real and fresh as if it had happened the day before; but I knew it didn't. I couldn't shake the feeling that the restaurant – that scene – had actually happened sometime long ago. It was impossible to separate the dream from any kind of remembered reality.

I got up, went to the bathroom, and looked at myself in the mirror. My feet were cold against the hard ceramic tile. My teeth chattered a bit, and I hugged myself to warm up. I had spent three years walking into a bathroom with radiant heated floors beneath imported slate. Now I stood in front of a medicine cabinet mirror, my face broken into two planes by a crack in the glass' lower right corner. My face looked tired. *Was that a new wrinkle?* My brown hair looked flat. Every cell in my body looked old.

I opened the medicine cabinet: empty. Most of my toiletries and make-up were still in a box marked "Bathroom" sitting on the toilet seat.

I was used to mornings by myself. Dennis would always wake up and leave while I was still in bed. He would hustle off to early meetings or waiting cabs to go to the airport. I was not a morning person, but I loved mornings alone.

After getting dressed in some light blue scrubs and a new pair of Keds, I brushed my hair back and put on makeup for work. I rarely did that. But I was single again.

I didn't have many rows left to knit on the hat I was making, but I grabbed my project bag anyway. I put it in my purse, and put on the warmest coat I owned, a down coat that I had taken from my mother the last time I was home, and my favorite scarf, a light blue wool and mohair blend done in a seed stitch. My walk to the PATH train took me past the library next to my apartment, across Church Square Park, around the corner past Patricia's Yarns and down Hudson Street. Like ants filing to the anthill, everyone in town seemed to be walking in the same direction toward the train station. Looking at them, I noticed most commuting Hobokenites were my age or slightly older. Most of the men wore suits and long overcoats; while, most of the women wore business attire.

I hustled through the turnstiles and made my way onto a waiting 33rd Street-bound train. I noticed the girl across the aisle from me. She had coffee. *I don't have coffee.* I was obviously new to this commute. I took out my knitting. I thought I would have a six-minute train ride to 14th Street. Not so. Middle of rush hour, the train screeched to a halt.

Commuters surrounding me looked about impatiently. Girls sipped their coffee. Men looked at their watches and heaved their chests. A woman across from me kept clicking her Blackberry wheel and typing furiously. Finally, she looked up, surprised, noticed we weren't moving, and laid her head backwards on the seat and closed her eyes. The train was tense. No one talked. I continued decreasing the hat.

"They said it was runnin' on time. I think it is." There was a man sitting next to me. He was clad in an army fatigue hat with a huge S on it. I don't know what that stood for. He was wearing a tan and orange t-shirt and some kind of nondescript trouser pants. He held a puffy black coat under his arms. He had a toothpick in his mouth.

The train idled, brakes sighing. The electric hum slowed and stopped. The conductor's voice came on: "We got a train ahead, we appreciate your patience. We'll get movin' shortly."

I continued working on the hat. Good thing I had it with me. I started getting nervous about being late for work. I had that little feeling in the pit of your stomach, a gnawing.

In moments of intense stress I knit. My knitting bag is always next to me on the subway. I used to commute uptown three times a week in college to help pay for school, but invariably subways were late. I'd be waiting at the uptown platform and three downtown trains would come. I would curse each one as it whizzed by. What a waste: three empty trains rolling by, while the uptown platform was filling to the brim. And even as my train finally came, a fourth downtown train would peek its' nose around the corner and I'd see its' lights. Already I'd be formulating the cursed excuses for my bosses uptown. They were nice and never said anything when I was late, but something about being late made me incredibly stressed. I could tell they were upset about my tardiness. "Sorry, the train was late." "Sorry, I can't believe how bad these trains are." "I left with plenty of time but the train was delayed *fifteen minutes.* It just sat there!" "Who ever invented the C Train?" "Public transportation. What are you going to do?"

But when I start knitting it's like I can create a sense of stasis. I'm just following a pattern, doing one stitch after the other and pretty soon I'm not thinking of anything at all.

The train lurched and we were moving again. The microphone squealed loudly. Half the train covered its ears. People were wincing. "Attention, ladies 'n gennlemen. Due to train traffic, we're goina hafta bypass 14th through 33rd Street. That's right, bypass 14th through 33rd Street. For local service get off at 9th Street and transfer UPTOWN to another train. Next stop, 9th Street. We appreciate your patience. 9th Street, next stop."

The train groaned. Inside and out. People let out a collective "arrrggghhh." More watch-checking, sighing.

I looked at the guy next to me. He shrugged. "Guess it's goin' to be late now. They done said it was goin' *on time* up to *33rd Street*, but now it's goin' *express*. I didn't hear no announcement; I was listening; I didn't hear them say nothin'; but *now* it must be goin' *express*."

"Yup," I said, and tried a little winsome smile. I focused on my knitting. I decreased one row.

"You'll get there." He kind of laughed or grunted and sort of looked content with himself. The toothpick bobbed up and down every time he talked.

His teeth were still sort of gritted together when he spoke, like he didn't really open his mouth. He wore huge aviator-frame spectacles that made his eyes look big.

"Yeah, I know. My stop is 14th Street but I'll have to probably walk up from Ninth or take the uptown if it's right there." He continued. "Just go on up to Ninth Street and go up and around," as he gestured with his arm, toothpick a-dangling, "and catch the local and you be all right."

"Right. Thanks."

The train rattled and I caught my reflection in the black window opposite. We picked up speed. We seemed to be moving pretty fast.

The guy spoke up. "Don't let it bother you none. Heh, heh. I used to let it bother me; *man* I used to get so *worked up* over it, I used to get *mad*. But I learned to not let it bother me none. Now I know I'll get there. If I have to take a roundabout way, I'll get there. You just choose your path, stay *alert*," both hands out straight now, gesturing, "choose the path, you'll get there."

"Right."

I was looking at him now, nodding assent or agreement or whatever, but he wasn't really looking at me. I got the sense that he wasn't really having the conversation with me. He was kind of looking straight out and still gesticulating with his two hands. "You understand? Now I just *maintain*."

I tried to pay attention to my knitting. He kept going on.

"You know, maintaining. Choose the path, keep going. I learn to not think too much about things. You think too much about some things, you liable to…to…think your head off! And you want to keep your head, don't you? Don't you?"

"Yes," I said with a smile, still trying to keep track of my stitches.

"Yes you *do*." He was talking straight out in front of him, nary a glance my way.

Finally the subway came to a stop at Ninth Street, and he reached out and gave me a good old high-five as I was leaving the car. I smiled again as my hand slapped his. He had that air of inevitability about him, like, as he starts talking to you, you go, "Ok, self, Ok. I knew this guy would be here," somehow. Like he was waiting for me. Like this guy does nothing all day but ride the subway or PATH train up and down from Manhattan to Hoboken and waits for people to tell his philosophies to. I bundled my nearly completed hat into my bag, stepped off the train and mounted the steps to the street.

So far, so good. My new commute seemed relatively easy.

The worst part about winter in the city is walking out of a subway station. Not because of the cold, but because the 30 seconds it takes to ascend the stairs blows your hair as if you went through a wind tunnel, and then when you hit the frozen street, the cold flash-freezes your hair in its I-just-stuck-my-hand-in-an-electrical-socket do. I caught a glimpse of myself in a darkened shop window as I got out onto the street, and my hair looked as if it had been styled by Albert Einstein. I reached my hands up to try to tame it.

My physical therapy office sits on the corner of 7th Ave. and 13th Street, in the heart of the West Village, one short block and one long block from the PATH. I hadn't seen any of my co-workers for days. I wondered if I would be able to just sneak into the office unnoticed, and start right in with a patient. I took the elevator up to the sixth floor.

When I opened the door to the office, I ran into Mark, who was standing just inside. He gave me a grave look. "Hi Jane."

"Hi Mark. Sorry, sorry I'm late."

"How are you doing?"

"I'm ok," I replied, still flattening my hair with my hands, hoping he had no further questions. "The PATH train, it got stuck in the tunnel and then it dropped me at Ninth so I had to walk up."

"The PATH Train? You live in Tribeca?"

"I did…I meant to be on time. After missing so many days. I left in plenty of time."

"It's OK, Jane. Don't worry about it. Were you sick?" He tilted his head and gave me a concerned look.

"I…" I did not want to start talking about it, but decided to just come right out with it.

"It's been a long weekend, Mark. Dennis and I broke up. I moved out... I moved to Hoboken."

"What? Really? Hoboken," he said. "It happened that fast?"

"I know," I said. "I'm still trying to wrap my head around it."

"What happened?"

Try as I might to stop it, I began to feel that all-too-familiar sadness. I began explaining, again, the events that caused me to call out of work. *Maybe I should just write this story down, run off copies, and hand it out to anyone who asks.* My coworkers started filing out of their offices to listen. They all hung on every word. Everyone gathered to hear *Jane's Break-up Story* around the desk of Angela, our receptionist. She lived for gossip like this.

I gave them a relatively shortened version (relative, that is, to the hour I was on the phone with my mother, or the nights I stayed up talking to Rachel) and "he cheated on me," was all they needed to hear.

"Let me know when you are ready to date again," Angela said callously when I finished. "I know some nice boys."

"Thanks," I said to Angela trying to be polite. I knew full well the boys Angela liked all had fake tans and lived at home with their mothers.

"Who's my first client today?" I asked to change the subject.

"Marvin," Angela said, looking at a clip board on her desk. "We had to change the schedule around because you were out last week." I noticed the other physical therapists walked away quickly when she said Marvin's name.

My terrible winter was officially worse! Marvin was the scourge of the office. He was cantankerous and opinionated and made comments like "what's wrong with you" or "hold my leg like *this*."

CURSE OF THE BOYFRIEND SWEATER

He was a cancer survivor who had endured months of chemo and radiation. The neuropathy in his legs caused chronic pain in his knees, ankles, and feet. I wanted to feel sorry for him, but he was never nice to anyone in the office. He always wore the same thing – a white oversized Yankees t-shirt and sweat pants. He was overweight, balding, and in his late fifties.

I tried to put on a good face as I opened the door to Room 1, the closest room to the elevator, the only room Marvin would go in.

"Hello Marvin. How are you feeling today?" I queried.

"Not too good," he said with his strong Bronx accent. "My feet are killing me and I had a long weekend, couldn't sleep."

"Believe me, I understand," I admitted.

He lay back on the bed and I began lifting his heavy legs.

"It's been a tough week for me," Marvin confided. "I got to move out of my apartment. They're kicking me out. I've been living there for twenty-two years. Twenty-two years, ya believe that!"

His apartment in Stuyvesant-town, a working class

housing unit on the east side of Manhattan, had been bought by developers – "rats," he called them.

"They're redoing the whole place; new walls, new windows, new units. They're driving the rents up when they finish, the rats. I can't afford it no more. I won't even be able to move back. They're trying to get these uppity NYU kids in with their parents to pay for it. They gave me my two month's notice. After everything I've been through, Vietnam, cancer, my wife…" he said, laying back on the examining table, covering his face with his right arm, "I just don't know what's comin' next."

"You'll be fine," I asserted as I gently lowered his left leg and picked up his right. I started to feel really bad for Marvin. "Now pull on this," I said and handed him a large elastic band, the other end of which I wrapped around his foot. "These exercises will help."

"That's beautiful," he said, peeking from under his arm.

"What is?"

"Your scarf," he said, now pointing at my neck. I didn't realize that I had left it on.

"Thank you. My mother knitted this for me." I touched it.

CURSE OF THE BOYFRIEND SWEATER

"My wife used to knit," he told me.

"I knit too. I've always loved to knit. Ever since I was a little girl." I added, "Even as an uppity NYU kid."

He looked at me. Then he got it and smiled. I told him that more and more young people, like me, were knitting, how it is very therapeutic. I explained that knitting helped me to de-stress, and how it is the one thing my mother and I loved to do together.

"Can you knit sweaters? My wife used to knit sweaters."

"I can," I replied.

It turned into the nicest session I had ever had with Marvin.

I helped Marvin hobble out of the office, holding his cane for him. When we got to the elevator door, he actually said, "Thank you, Jane."

When the elevator door opened I stood face to face with a cute bicycle delivery boy. He was tall with dark hair and light eyes. Instead of a winter coat, he was wearing a heavy wool sweater and jeans with one pant leg rolled up. He looked like a model from Abercrombie and Fitch standing in the elevator next to his Italian bicycle. *He's beautiful.*

"Jane?" he questioned. *How did he know my name?*

I paused, still staring directly at him. *He has great eyes.*

"I'm looking for Jane Sullivan. Do you know who that is?" He raised his eyebrows waiting for me to respond and stepped out of the elevator.

"…I'm Jane," I finally said and smiled back at him. It had been a while since I had even looked at another man.

"Delivery," he said and held out a small white envelope. He asked me to sign a wrinkled piece of paper that he pulled out from his front pocket.

Marvin, impatient from waiting and standing in the elevator, said, "Going down!" and closed the elevator door on the delivery boy – his bike still inside! You could hear Marvin laugh as the elevator descended.

"Dammit!" exclaimed the messenger. He tried repeatedly pressing the elevator button.

"Sorry about that," I said, trying not to laugh. "The stairs are right there," pointing to the exit sign. He snatched the paper back from my hands and ran to the stairwell.

I opened the envelope. Inside was the necklace I had deliberately left on the nightstand at Dennis's place. He had given it to me on my birthday. At the time, I was hoping for an engagement ring. Stuck to the necklace was a yellow Barnes & Ross sticky note, with a message written in Dennis's perfect cursive: "I wanted you to have this when I gave it to you. Call if you want."

Call if you want?

"That's beautiful," Angela said, looking at the necklace as I walked back into the office.

"You like it?" I said, "it's yours," and dropped it onto her desk.

Chapter 8: Room 205

It didn't take long to settle into my new life. I found Empire Coffee Co., the same place where the regular customers of Patricia's Yarns get their coffee, a great spot for morning lattes. Each day the 9 blocks I walked between my apartment and the PATH got easier and easier, despite the slushy snow that narrowed the sidewalks. I was so busy at work that the only knitting I could do was finishing the hat I purchased at Patricia's. And even that I knitted mostly waiting for and/or sitting on the train.

Friday morning found me doing just that: standing on the PATH platform, engrossed in the hat that was almost finished.

I heard a voice behind me. "Jane, right?" I turned around to see Michelle.

"Hello!" I answered. Michelle's long blond hair was tucked beneath a dark green wool hat. "It's nice to see you again. How are you?" I asked over the noise of the oncoming train.

"I'll be better when Spring arrives," she said loudly with a big smile.

We entered the train and sat down next to each other. "I'm going to go to knit night tonight at Trish's. Would you like to join me?" she asked.

"That sounds great!" I told her, astonished by my good fortune running into her.

"Excellent. It's at seven."

"Should I bring anything?" I asked.

"Just yourself," she replied.

I was so excited to get to the shop that night that my time with clients seemed to last twice as long. My last client ran late that day, so I didn't have time to make it home after work. Instead, I went straight to Patricia's Yarns. I thought I was on time, but I could hear laughter coming from inside before I even opened the door.

"What can Margaux bring?" Patricia asked a group of people as I walked into the room. Patricia's hand was holding the telephone out for everyone to talk.

"More wine!" laughed one of the girls.

"Cheddar cheese!" announced another.

"Dark chocolate…" exclaimed another voice to the approval of all.

"Did you get all that?" Patricia said into the phone with a laugh.

The room had felt large when I had visited the shop before; now, with everyone crowded around the table, laden with knitting needles and yarn, it felt like a dining room at Thanksgiving.

Michelle got up from her seat at the table and stood next to me. "Everyone, this is Jane," she said.

I was greeted to a chorus of "Hi Jane." I felt as if I was attending a twelve-step program, except everyone was smiling and laughing.

"Hi...everyone," I said with a little wave, slightly embarrassed.

With the group laughing and talking, Michelle did her best to introduce me. She pointed to the people sitting around the large table as she talked. "This is Anna, this is P.A. – er, Jess – this is the other Jess, Doctor Doctor."

"Hi," said one Jess.

"Hi," said the other.

Michelle pointed, " – this is Jamison, David, and Heather."

"Hey guys," came a loud voice from the open door behind us.

"Margaux!" everyone exclaimed in return.

Margaux entered the shop carrying a plastic bag in one hand and holding up a large bottle of wine in the other, the kind with a little rooster on the label.

"Here, Jane, take a seat," Patricia said, and pulled out a chair from the table. "Let me get a bottle opener," she said to Margaux, multitasking, and took the wine from her hands.

"Thanks," I said sheepishly as I sat down amid the boisterous group. .

By the time Margaux, Michelle, and Patricia sat down, the table seemed too small for the nine of us, but no one seemed to mind.

Although I tried, I couldn't remember all of the names. So I turned to a person I knew. "Patricia," I said. "I don't have a project to work on tonight. Any suggestions? What is everyone here making?"

"Socks," said David. Being the only male, I remembered his name easily. He held up a bright orange skein of yarn. David was a big presence at the table. He had shoulder-length hair and a scruffy goatee. He was wearing a huge brown sweater that I later found out he knitted himself. He sat at the head of the table with his legs crossed. His big fingers diligently worked a super-fine fingering weight yarn.

"I'm making a shrug," said Anna in what I later discovered was a New Zealand accent. Anna was a petite, pretty girl with a short bob hair-cut and a cheerleader's smile. Anna held up the beginning of a very cute shrug made from bulky wool. "It's knitting up quickly," she said.

"Hopefully, this will be a baby blanket," said a girl with long black hair and a big smile. I couldn't remember her name. "Heather," she reminded me. She reached her hand to mine. "Nice to meet you," she said.

"I'm also making a baby blanket," said a tall, curly-haired girl who sat very upright in her chair. She showed me a gorgeous square made of variegated yarns.

"Sorry – I know you're Jess, but are you P.A., or Doctor Doctor?" I responded.

"P.A.," she said.

"I'm Doctor Doctor," replied a smaller, red-haired girl. "Since we're both Jessica, they gave us nicknames."

"Doctor Doctor is our smarty pants," said Patricia. "She is studying for her Ph.D. *and* M.D.. P.A. stands for physician's assistant. The nicknames help us keep the Jessicas straight."

"I'm knitting a hat for my boyfriend," Doctor Doctor said bashfully.

"So there's P.A. Jess and Doctor Doctor..." I said, trying to get it straight. "Got it. And you are Jamison," I said to the girl sitting directly across the table from me. Her short hair was tucked under a knit beret. She was wearing a T-shirt that said, *"Knitting is Knotty."*

"Yes, very nice to meet you. I'm trying to knit a sweater, but I've frogged it twice," Jamison said with a smile and a laugh.

"So what are you thinking about making?' Patricia asked.

I wasn't sure. But the group was happy to help. David, in particular, started telling me about his favorite projects: which ones were easy, which ones had patterns that didn't work, which ones looked beautiful but took "forever" to finish. I finally settled on a hand-painted yarn called Koigu.

Koigu, I would later learn, is a very small company, and all their yarns are hand-dyed by only three people. I had heard of it before and seen it in magazines, but never held it.

Each Koigu skein was beautiful and the number of options was overwhelming. I settled on one that was dyed in a dark rainbow. I loved it in the hank, and when Patricia balled it for me it looked amazing. The yarn went from navy to a deep burgundy to forest green and felt wonderful in my hands. I knew it would make a great pair of socks.

I had gone to other shops' knit nights before –a few in the suburbs with my mom, which were fun, but most of the conversations were about mortgages, husbands, soccer, or coupons. They were relatively boring. I also had gone to one in New York. There, too, I didn't have a great time. All of the girls were coworkers and rarely talked to me.

That wasn't how it was at Patricia's. Everyone was close to my age or slightly older and everyone, like me, loved to knit. Some had recently learned to knit at the shop under Patricia's guidance, while others had been knitting for a long time.

"Did you guys hear what happened to Margaux?" asked Patricia.

"O.k. But, let me tell it," replied Margaux, getting out of her seat, gaining the attention of the room. "So you all know I work at a Catholic school, right? Well, this morning, I'm walking to my car – I parked like ten blocks from my apartment – parking in this town sucks – and I'm trying to open my car door, but it is totally frozen shut. So, I'm pulling on the door, pulling like this," she starts lurching her body from front to back. "And my hand slips off the handle and I fly backwards, ass-first into a snow bank!"

"Oh my," I said, over the laughter of others.

"But that wasn't the worst part of my day! No, no. No, the real problem," said Margaux, "was that I didn't know I had ripped my tights. And, that day, I had to meet with a girls' group to talk about our school's *dress code*."

"I guess they noticed," said David, trying not to laugh.

"They did, but I didn't realize it until I was walking out of the classroom, and all of the girls were laughing as I walked away. I apparently had a giant rip down my backside," she motioned from her ankles to her butt.

"I just keep laughing thinking about all the people that walked past you this morning while you were ass-first in a snow bank," Patricia laughed.

"Thanks," said Margaux, trying not to laugh as well. "And no one helped me!"

"Awwww," replied the group.

The two hours seemed like minutes. At nine a man knocked on the shop door.

"Adam!" exclaimed Margaux, obviously after a few glasses of wine.

Patricia unlocked the door and kissed him. "Hi everyone," he said.

"Adam, this is Jane," said Patricia. "Jane, this is my husband, Adam. Adam, you know everyone else."

"Hi everybody," he waved.

"Nice to meet you," I said.

"Ok, time to clean up," said Patricia clapping her hands to the group.

"Anyone up for a drink at L and J's?" asked David.

"I can only go for one, I've got to work tomorrow," said Jamison.

"I'm in," said Margaux.

"Sure," said Doctor Doctor, "but only one."

"We're in," exclaimed Adam.

"Go on then," replied Anna in her kiwi accent.

Heather and P.A. Jessica said goodnight; both had to get home to "little ones". The rest of us walked a short, but bitter cold block, and stepped down below street level into a cozy tavern called L and J's. Adam and David went straight to the bar to order drinks. The girls settled into a table by the window facing Washington Street.

L and J's wasn't like many of the bars or clubs I would go to in New York City. It was a locals' bar. Blues music played just loud enough to hear over the patrons' voices. There was only one TV, and it was playing old movies on loop. In fact the whole place gave off an ambience of cinephilia, with black and white star photos of Audrey Hepburn, Humphrey Bogart, and, of course, Hoboken's own Frank Sinatra adorning the walls. The bartender was friendly and greeted us immediately when we walked in. He wore blue jeans and a black CBGB's shirt. My guess was that he had seen the knitters walk in numerous times before. All the girls took out their knitting at the table and picked up right where they had left off at knit night.

Adam and David brought glasses of red wine to us two at a time. The boys drank pints of Guinness. David sipped his and said, "So Jane, how are you enjoying your first knit night?"

"I'm having a great time!"

"Ah yes." His expression grew wistful. "I remember my first knit night in Hoboken." He took another sip of frothy beer.

"That's nothing compared to the first time I met Doctor Doctor in the shop," interrupted Patricia. "Oh my god, I remember this," giggled Anna.

"Jess," said Patricia impishly, "do you recall?"

"Uh, YEAH!" Said Doctor Doctor.

"What happened?" I asked, eager to hear.

"So," Patricia began, turning to me, "I am sitting in the shop on a quiet Saturday morning and in walks a bubbly, curly-haired girl wearing these cute glasses."

"They were cute, huh?" said Doctor Doctor.

"Yes," said Patricia getting back to the story. "So I say hello – asked if there was anything I can help her find – she says she is just browsing. So I said take your time and if you have any questions let me know. So away she walks to look around. Then she walked back to the counter, and said 'Well, I am *here* because I cannot be in my apartment right now. See, I am looking for a new roommate as mine is moving out and I have someone coming to view the apartment in…ohh…15 minutes…mm hmm…right, so why am I here? Well around 11:30 this morning I reminded my current roommate that someone was coming to view the apartment at 1, and then I went downstairs to grab a coffee. I came back up to the living room to sit with my morning cup-o'-joe. I'm trying to study, some time passes. Next thing, I hear

CURSE OF THE BOYFRIEND SWEATER

her and her boyfriend beginning to move around from her room to the bathroom and back - so I think that is great. They will vacate so I can show the new potential roommate. But no! No, no, no – not great. The next sounds I hear are the bed "rockin'" as they are totally going at it. Seriously! ...So here I am. I just cannot believe this! Can you believe this? I am trying to rent out this share and it is currently being 'used' - ugghh!'"

"Oh no!" I said with a laugh.

Doctor Doctor laughed. "I didn't know what else to do. I was walking around Hoboken, banished from the apartment, and saw Trish's shop. I had to go somewhere!"

Trish said, "And so that is how we met! I remembered her for a long time after as the girl who came in while her roommate was getting lucky."

"I've never heard that story," said David. "That's pretty funny."

"Anyway, I can now thank my ex-roommate for my love of knitting and my new friends," said Doctor Doctor. "To knitting," she said holding up her wine glass.

"Cheers" I said with a laugh, my glass meeting hers.

By the time I was ready to go, my teeth were purple from red wine, I only had one sock half-knit, and I had to rub my cheeks they hurt so much from laughing.

Walking home, my cell phone rang. The caller ID told me it was from the 201 area code. *Who's in 201?* It must have been the wine, because I never would've picked up otherwise.

"Hello?"

"Hello," said the caller.

"Dad? Where are you calling from?"

"Secaucus," he responded. "Jane, do you have a minute?"

"What time is it?" I asked, trying my best to sound sober.

"11:30," he said.

"Dad, what is it?"

"Jane, I'm at a hotel."

"For business?" I asked. My father worked for the Turnpike Authority. He rarely traveled for work, unless it was down the highway fifteen minutes to the border of Essex and Union County.

"Not exactly," he said.

I was almost home. I stopped on the second flight of stairs that led to the hallway of my apartment. I had two stairs to go.

"Your mother and I had a big argument," he said in a quiet tone and paused waiting for a response. The silence felt like it lasted hours. I dangled off the banister. The stairs swam beneath me. My contacts felt fuzzy. I blinked to try to moisten them.

"Jane, it's going to be ok. I wanted to call you and tell you so that you hear it from me," he said.

"What kind of argument?"

"One that caused me to walk out."

"Dad…" I think I sounded drunk.

"You can get in touch with me at the number I called you from. I'm in Room 205," he continued. "Jane, are you listening?"

"You moved out, Dad?"

There was silence on the other end. He sighed. "I don't know if it's permanent." He paused. "Your mother and I…" He fell silent again.

He moved out? I pictured him sitting in some dank hotel room, next to the receiver on his bedside table.

"Whatever happens, I want you to know that I love you, Janie."

"I love you too…" I whispered back. I was upset and confused.

"Listen. Get some rest. It's late. Call me and we can talk about this. Room 205."

"Bye," I whispered. *Room 205.*

I stood on the step. It wasn't until a Chinese food delivery boy pushed his way past me up the stairs that I decided to follow him up and go into my apartment.

"Come see me?" I texted Rachel as I fell asleep.

Chapter 9: Straight from Moscow

Two years before. March.

"Barnes and Ross was started in 1997 by two <u>Cornell</u> alums who sang in a Cornell *<u>a cappella</u>* group and were members of <u>Beta Beta Tzi Upsilon</u>, the only four-letter Greek organization on American campuses. In its first year, after landing a major contract with <u>Mack's Body Wash</u> (*'Mack it to the Max – With Mack's'*), and seeing not only a spike in its revenue and market share, but a revolutionizing of the <u>man-grooming industry</u> nationwide, Barnes and Ross became a premier ad agency. Barnes and Ross specialized in anything pertaining to what might fall under the 'fraternal experience,' and found a real niche with American college-age and recently graduated males. The co-founders, now retired (at ages 39 and 40, respectively), were Mr. <u>Matthew Barnes</u> of <u>Pittsburgh, PA</u>, and Mr. <u>Alexander Ross</u>, of <u>Concord, MA</u>. Nowadays Mr. <u>Dennis Laight</u> is Vice President in charge of development.

In the past five years, Barnes and Ross has quintupled its previous market share, diversified, and even bought a slightly older but still fledgling ad agency, which purchase brought with it the contracts to <u>The Nordic Experience Home and Office Sauna Line</u> and <u>The Odyssean Do-It-Yourself Bedmaker's Kits.</u> <u>Penelope Cruz</u> is featured in their commercials reclining on beds. Matt Barnes joked that they "really hit a homer" with the acquisition.[citation needed] <u>Bjorn</u>

Borg, long in retirement from professional tennis, coincided his first appearance back at Wimbledon in 20 years with an appearance in The Nordic Experience's first post-merger commercial line, in which he is clad in what appears to be only a towel, and delivers a sincere monologue to the camera during a slow and steamy zoom-in on the merits of the Sauna for Home and Office. This commercial series was designed specifically for the 2008 Wimbledon Championship, and subsequently aired on ESPN, FOX, The Tennis Channel, The Golf Channel, CBS, and NBC. The Nordic Experience opened eight new U.S. offices in August of 2008. The Offices of Barnes and Ross, Ltd., now relocated from 119th St. to Varick Street in lower Tribeca, boast three separate sauna facilities, one on each floor."

So read the Wikipedia entry on Dennis's company.

"Isn't it great, Janie?" Dennis liked to call me Janie after I told him that's the nickname my dad used . I told him that on our third date, after he called me "Janie", and he seemed to really like the idea of calling me the same name as my dad . (Something like: Dennis: "Blah blah blah, Janie, blah blah blah." Me: "Tee-hee, that's what my dad calls me." Dennis: "Hot.") It's probably the nickname that stuck the most with Dennis. Sometimes he preferred Jane-o. Other times, Jane-tendo. In summer he called me Janie-Freckleface. I never liked that.

CURSE OF THE BOYFRIEND SWEATER

Dennis had been at the office until well after midnight, but had just arrived home. A tousled untucked shirt hung half-buttoned off of him. I stared at the back of his head as he read me the entry from his 27" Apple computer screen. I was sleepy and had been awakened, but was glad to see him. I got out of bed and walked up next to him. I looked at the screen. There was the Wikipedia entry, Barnes and Ross logo emblazoned in jpeg pixels on the upper right.

"Did you check the blue line sub nomine de yours truly's? That's right, Mr. Denny has his own Wiki entry. I'm loving this. Look at this. It's new."

Dennis clicked on a link. We were diverted to the Barnes & Ross website's trailer section. It was a TV spot for the Thor Brand Pro Hand-Tool Line. It was a bunch of guys lined up in a row with assorted hand tools and dressed in a variety of costumes including popped collars, plaid shorts, riding horses holding polo clubs and riding crops, etc. The gag was that they were supposed to be a "pro-tool line" of their own; i.e. a line of "professional tools". They were the marketing representatives for the brand. Dennis clicked the link and a voice came on: "Now *that's* a Professional Tool-Bag; drill like a pro with Thor's Pro Tool Line." I always thought the line of tool-bags was kind of funny and, frankly, emblematic of all the guys Dennis worked with. Though I had to admit, the ads were really pretty good.

"Dennis, it's funny."

"Yeah, I know, babe."

"Are you coming to bed?"

"Not just yet. Actually, gotta head out again in a minute. A little wired. Meeting a client late night. Also, might not be in tomorrow night again until late."

"Really?"

"Yeah, yeah, you know, got to keep the old coal fires burning. Gotta pay Yolanda's salary."

"OK, Dennis. I'm going back to bed."

"But Jane."

"Yeah?" I said, groggy, clawing back the covers.

"Here." He took out a tiny box from his pants pocket.

I opened it. Inside was a thin bracelet with two stones – one gray, one green attached to it. "Dennis, this is beautiful. What is this?"

"Oh, just a little something. I picked it up for you special."

"Where did you get this?"

"Eh…" He scratched his head. "Doesn't matter. Let's just say you won't be finding this bracelet in any old store."

"Dennis, this is so sweet."

"Sure, sure. The two stones – it's like our favorite colors, you know? Gray for you, green for me?"

"Dennis…" I got back out of bed and went over to Dennis to give him a big kiss goodnight.

***

Head throbbing, I reached for my phone on the bedside table. It was blinking yellow and red. The yellow told me my battery was almost dead. The red was a text from Rachel. "Ok," it said.

Ok what? I clutched my forehead and wracked my brain for what had happened the night before. Slowly it all came back: knit night, red wine, the call from Dad, news of their separation, collapsing into bed, and a text to Rachel to meet me.

I looked at the clock. It was past 11am. Sun flooded the apartment. I never closed the curtains the night before. *Why had I been dreaming about Dennis?* Why, all of a sudden, after so many nights not thinking about him?

PATRICIA AND ADAM SCRIBNER

My head surged. Thank goodness it was Saturday. I fell out of bed, put on a pot of coffee, and collapsed back on top of my sheets.

I rubbed my forehead with my hand. *How could my parents be married for twenty-eight years and decide now to call it quits? Why is everything happening at once?*

I must have dozed off, since a loud buzzing nearly made me jump out of my skin. It was my intercom. I rolled back out of bed to answer the bell.

"Who is it?" I groaned, half-awake.

"Open the door, it's friggin' freazing!" the intercom buzzed back.

"Hi Rachel, come on up," I replied with a smile, and walked to the door to greet her. I rested my head on the closed door until I heard her footsteps.

"You look awful," she said, bursting into the room all bright and cheery. *I hate morning people.*

Rachel looked great. Her curly brown hair shaped her high cheekbones perfectly. She was wearing a Burberry coat over a stylish skirt and blouse. A chunky necklace of deep blue stones hung around her neck. She was in boots with heels despite the snow outside. I was wearing PJ's and slippers - and was perfectly content to stay in them.

"Get dressed, we're going for brunch," she said. "You ok?"

"I'll tell you at brunch," I replied. "Help yourself to coffee."

I took a quick shower – which, combined with a cup of coffee, did wonders for my head. I got dressed and ready to leave.

"Oh wait," I said. "I have something for you." I went back into my bedroom and grabbed a project bag. "It's a surprise," I told her.

We went to brunch at a little restaurant just off Washington Street, the main street of Hoboken. Trish had recommended Anthony David's to me as soon as I met her, and I had heard the girls at knit night talk about it. Like Patricia's shop and so many of the other quaint shops in town, it had large glass Victorian windows. Wooden chairs and tables with small flower arrangements in the middle sat neatly between displays of imported coffee beans, artisanal cheeses, and freshly baked baguettes. The restaurant smelled like deep roast coffee and bacon. I ordered the frittata with fresh mozzarella and basil. Rachel had an egg-white spinach omelet.

"So what's going on with you? Are you doing better?" asked Rachel.

"*I* am, but my *parents* aren't," I said.

I told her about the phone call from my father the night before. I told her I wasn't sure of the reasons or the details – my parents were being awfully cagey about the whole thing – but that I was upset at my father for walking out.

"They're grown-ups. They should know how to settle things rationally," I concluded.

"Are *you* doing ok?" she asked again.

"Up until last night's phone call, I was doing better than ok – at least better than I thought I would be."

I gave Rachel the rundown on my time in Hoboken, my new friends, even my recent work with Marvin. I told her I loved having my own place and that after one week, I was sleeping alone without thinking about Dennis…at least not too much.

"You're not too lonely in your new city?"

"Well, I've actually met quite a few people." I said.

Rachel smiled. "Oh yeah?"

"Yeah, the girls over at the knitting shop. You would really love them. You have to come spend some time with me there."

"Absolutely. I will," she replied. "I miss having you in the city, though."

"Oh please," I said. "As if you don't have plenty to do without me."

"Well, I just hope you don't move any further away than you already have. There's no way I'm getting on NJ Transit!"

"Rachel. You know I'm only 20 minutes from your apartment. And oh yeah –" I smiled a little secretive smile and reached into my purse. "I made this for you."

I took out the off-white hat, knit in berry stitch. "I love it so much," I said, looking it over one last time, "I almost kept it for myself." I handed it to her.

"I love it too!" she exclaimed. Right away she tried it on, fitting it over her curly locks.

"Look at the inside," I said excitedly.

She took off the hat and read the label I had sewn to the inside. "This garment was handmade with love for <u>Rachel</u>." She put the hat back on. "Awww! You're so sweet! How's it look?"

"Beautiful," I replied.

She took it off and gazed at it. "And it's white. Everyone knows how perfect you need to make the stitches on a white hat." She held it out in front of her. "Look at these berry stitches! So gorgeous."

She put it back on her head, centering it. The waitress dropped off the check at our table. "Let me pay for this one," I said.

"I feel like it's my birthday!" Rachel replied.

"I just want to thank you for all you've done."

By the time we left the restaurant it was afternoon. We strolled down Washington Street together, looking into the boutiques. Rachel, the self-proclaimed "Queen of Shopping," was carrying three new shopping bags by the time we reached First Street. I, on the other hand, didn't buy a thing. (After putting my new bed on my credit card, I decided buying anything other than yarn was out of the question.)

I hugged Rachel at the entrance to the PATH station and thanked her for a great afternoon. Later on, I texted her: "Thanks so much for coming to jersey! You're the best!"

"I had fun. Love the hat," Rachel responded. "Jersey Shmerzy – it's growing on me."

On the way home, I made one more stop at Trish's shop. I opened the door to be greeted by a little baby in a stroller. P.A. Jessica sat in a chair in the middle of the shop, pushing the baby girl back and forth. A yarn twisted up from a ball at P.A.'s feet into a tangle in her lap. Hanna, only 7 months old, was gazing at all of the vivid colors of yarn surrounding her. Her eyes were big and wide, blue and watery, and it seemed like with each push of the stroller she flipped them from one shelf to the next. I sat down at the table next to them. Patricia was behind the counter on the phone. She gave me a wave hello.

"Future knitter?" I asked P.A.

"You bet," P.A. said. "She loves coming in here – all the colors."

"Did you knit that for her?" I pointed to the intricate baby dress Hanna sported. It was rainbow-colored and done in a gorgeous lace stitch.

"I did, I did. All throughout my pregnancy. It practically took me all nine months."

I sat and began to knit. As Hanna fell asleep, P.A. started weaving in the ends of the baby blanket she had been working on. She moved to the table to join me, and gave the middle chair back to Riley, the Yorkie terrier. He hopped up onto the chair, spun around, and settled down. With little jerky movements of his head, he watched us knit.

My socks were a few decreases from completion when the door opened and in walked a man. Behind him three paces was a blond woman, who shut the door behind them.

Before Patricia had a chance to greet them, the man announced to us "My wife would like to knit."

The woman was a tall blond with streaks of black stretching from the roots of her hair. She was pretty, with tight lips and narrow eyes, but a demure chin and high cheekbones. She was wearing a lot of makeup. A strong perfume hung in the air around her. She waved shyly to us.

Patricia looked at us, like *who is this guy?* She asked the woman, "Have you knitted before?"

The woman looked from Patricia to her husband. He answered for her, "She has not. What do you have in this place for beginners?"

"Well," Patricia said, "there are lots of things a beginner can do. What are you thinking about knitting?" she asked the woman.

Again, instead of responding, she looked to her husband. He replied for her, "How about a sweater?"

"A sweater is a very advanced project. I wouldn't recommend it unless you've done a few smaller projects. What about a scarf?"

"Sure, sounds good." He shoved Riley off the chair and took a seat. "Honey," he said, very slowly, to his wife, "pick out a color you want." She looked a little confused. "Pick—" he gesticulated with each word "—a—color." He was miming taking a yarn from the wall. He looked at us. "Sorry, Russian. She doesn't speak any English yet. I just got her."

"*Got* her?" I asked.

"Yeah, hon. She's my bride. Straight from Moscow. Right?" He smiled at his wife. "My little *debushka*."

"*Devushka*," she responded quietly.

"Right, *devushka*. Damnit, always mess that up. Russian, hard language, you know?"

"Right, I'm sure," Patricia said, looking over at us wide-eyed.

I stood up. "I've used that yarn before, and love it," pointing to cubbies of Rowan Cocoon, the same yarn I used to make Rachel's hat.

"Who are you? You work here?" he asked.

"No…" I said, taken aback. "I…"

"Jane is an excellent knitter," Patricia said. "I would trust her recommendations."

"OK," he said. "Sure."

Meanwhile, Riley was pacing in a huff at the man's feet, angry his naptime had been interrupted. He barked once at the man.

"Whoa! Little dog, chill!" the guy said.

"Don't mind Riley," Trish said. "He doesn't bite. You're just in his usual spot."

"Want your spot back?" The man leaned down to address the dog. "Too bad! Ha ha ha ha!" He started cracking up. Riley looked at him confused.

"This yarn is great for beginners. Do you want me to ring you up?" Trish said, hurrying behind the counter with the wool I had suggested.

"I'm not so sure I like that yarn too much," he said. "I want to pick out a different one."

"Ok," she said as patiently as possible.

"Yeah, a different one." He stood up. Riley took the opportunity to jump back into the chair.

"OK," Trish said again.

"I'll let my wife choose, thank you." He gestured to his wife, still confused, to pick out another yarn.

"*Tak, shto dyelat?*" she asked her husband.

"Pick a yarn!" he yelled at her.

"Uh. Sir," Patricia didn't know what to say.

Jess and I stared at him in disbelief.

"What?" The guy looked at Jess and me.

"OK." He jumped up. "We're out of here." He grabbed his wife by the arm and led her out the door.

"No po-chemu?" she said as they hustled out.

"Because!" he answered. And they were gone.

We all looked at one another. Jess covered her mouth with her hand. Patricia picked up and hugged Riley.

"Yikes!" I finally said when they were far enough away.

Trish just stared after them, holding Riley, shaking her head.

"I can't believe some women actually live with people like that," said Jess.

"Every day," responded Patricia.

"Can you believe the way he talked to her?" asked Jess.

"It's terribly sad," I said, still in shock. "But yes."

"People can be so manipulative and controlling," said Jess.

"Men can be manipulative," I responded.

"Sometimes, women allow them to be. Though I am not sure *she* had much of a choice," replied Patricia. "You see that, and it makes you appreciate the good relationships in your life."

"Absolutely," said Jess. "That poor girl."

I stood up from my chair and started walking around the room. My mind immediately turned to my parents.

I was touching the yarn and samples. I saw a gray-colored lace-weight cowl lying in a trunk near the back of the shop. I pulled it out and unfolded it. The cowl was simple, but elegant. It was pretty, and delicate, like a beautiful web spun by a gray spider.

"This is stunning," I said quietly, to myself, not knowing if anyone heard me.

"Thank you," replied Patricia.

"I love it. Is there a pattern for it?" I asked, turning towards her.

"Yes. I have it somewhere on my computer." Patricia walked to her laptop. "Do you want it?"

"Hmm. No. Maybe I'll try writing one."

Patricia smiled at me approvingly. "You got it. But it's here if you need it."

"Which yarn did you use?" I asked.

Patricia walked me to a long row of mohair yarn. The skeins were arranged in a perfect rainbow. One at a time I took the skeins from their cubby and held them up to my neck in front of a mirror. The yarn was called Superior – one touch and I knew why. I chose the same gray Patricia had used for her cowl. I thought it would look great with my mother's fair Irish complexion.

"Nice choice," she said with a smile.

I hadn't designed the pattern yet, so I was unsure how many skeins I needed. I bought two, but was hoping I could eke out a cowl from one.

I called my mother as soon as I returned home, ready with great tidings of my new life in Hoboken. I was also ready to talk about Dad, hopeful that they had patched things up after my father's – I thought a bit drastic – move out. But the conversation did not go as I had hoped.

"Have you spoken to Dad?" I asked.

"Not since last Thursday," she replied in a soft voice.

"He's staying at a hotel," I told her.

"News to me."

"You mean he didn't tell you?"

"I think there are lots of things he never told me."

"What's that supposed to mean?"

"Lots of things we haven't told each other."

"Mom, please tell me what happened."

"I'm not sure," she said. "I came home from work on Friday and he was already packed." Her already soft voice began to shake.

"He said you had had a fight."

"We did."

"Mom, it's going to be fine. You and Dad will be able to work this out."

"I'm not so sure, honey. Oh – I'm getting a call. I have to go."

"Can't it wait?"

"No I need to get this."

"Who is it?"

There was a pause. "It's about our finances."

"You mean a lawyer? Mom, are you and Dad getting divorced?"

"Honey, I need to go, ok?"

"Fine. Ok. You know you can call me anytime if you need to talk, though," I said.

"Thank you, sweetheart. You too. I know this is hard for you. Just – I have to take this. Bye-bye."

***

On Sunday, I woke up to falling snow. The snow was an excuse to stay home – as if I needed one. I hadn't spent a full day in my new apartment since I moved in. I spent the afternoon cutting out new sticky-backed liners for my cabinets, stocking my toiletries in their appointed garrisons, and removing the last of my miscellaneous stuff from their boxes. While doing so, I found a small box with my scrawl in Sharpie that read: "Pictures." It was filled with photos of Dennis and me. One was of us having dinner by the sea at sunset on our trip to the Bahamas. Another was from the Hamptons, Dennis shirtless making a peace sign to the camera. There were a couple of pictures from the time I went with him on a business trip to Spain. And then there was one simply with him on the couch, reading the newspaper. I looked at that photo for a while. Then I looked up at my new apartment. I took the box, walked it down the stairs, and placed it on the curb outside with the trash. Flakes of snow fell gently from the sky and slowly covered the box.

RACHEL'S HAT

Rachel's Hat

Rachel's hat is a fitted or slouchy beret pattern. It is knit in the round and works up quickly on larger needles. Cocoon is a soft yarn made of alpaca & merino fibers, a wonderful blend to keep you warm on cool winter nights.

CURSE OF THE BOYFRIEND SWEATER

Yarn: Rowan Cocoon, 1 ball as written, or 2 for a more slouchy look.
Gauge: 14 stitches over 4 inches in Berry Stitch
Needles: Size US 10.5 (or size needed to get gauge)

Berry Stitch (multiple of 4 stitches):
Round 1 – Purl
Round 2 – P3tog, K1-P1-K1 in the same stitch – repeat until end of round.
Round 3 – Purl
Round 4 – K1-P1-K1 in the same stitch, P3tog – repeat until end of round.
Repeat these 4 rounds for pattern.

For abbreviations, please see list at end of book.

Instructions:
CO: 70 sts. Join for working in the round being careful not to twist. Work in Garter Stitch (K1 rnd, P1rnd) or K1P1 Ribbing for 1.5 inches.
Increase Row: *Kfb, K1, Kfb, Kfb, K1, Kfb, K1, Kfb* – repeat until the last 6 stitches: K1, Kfb, K1, Kfb, K2 – 112 stitches remain.

Work Berry Stitch until you have 5 inches (6 inches for a more slouchy look) from CO edge – ending with Purl row.

Decrease 48 stitches.

Row: K2 tog, k1, k3tog, k1, in the next round64sts rem

Work one full Berry Stitch repeat ending with a purl row.

Next decrease: K2 tog around 32 stitches remain,
Next Round: Purl
Next Round: P3tog, K1-P1-K1 in the same stitch around
Next Round: Purl
Decrease by K2tog around: 16 stitches remain
Purl 1 round
Decrease K2tog around: 8 stitches remain.

Cut yarn and pull through remaining loops. Weave in ends and wear!

CURSE OF THE BOYFRIEND SWEATER

ELLEN'S COWL

Ellen's Cowl

A simple, but elegant cowl pattern that utilizes a soft and luxurious yarn made of silk and cashmere.

Yarn: Superior by Filatura Di Crosa Golden Line
Needles: US 6 - 16" or 24" circular

For abbreviations, please see list at end of book.

Loosely cast on 100 stitches. Place marker & join for working in the round being careful not to twist stitches.

Work 6 rounds in garter stitch (knit 1 round & purl 1 round).
Knit in Stockinette Stitch for about 21" & finish off with 6 rounds garter stitch.

Bind off very loosely - consider using a larger needle in your right hand to make the bind off as flexible as possible.

Sew in your ends with a tapestry needle.

Chapter 10: Losing Count

I woke up earlier than usual on Monday- *without an alarm*- but stayed in bed finishing my socks before getting in the shower for work. Just one more row, I kept thinking.

On the way to the office, I bought a café mocha from Empire Coffee and bagels for everyone from my favorite bagel place on 14th Street in the city.   I took the stairs instead of the elevator to my office floor. When I walked in, I saw Angela wearing the necklace I had dropped on her desk.

"I love it," she said, clutching it.

"I picked up bagels," I announced to anyone who was listening. Three of my co-workers came out of their offices.

"Whaaaaat? Did you get lucky this weekend?" asked Angela with a deviant look.

I smiled. "No, I'm just trying to be in a good mood," I said. "Can't I get bagels for the office?"

"You sure can," said Mark walking into the reception area. "Thanks. Save me one, I have Mrs. Etter coming in two minutes."

"Who do I have today?" I asked Angela.

"Jane, you have Mrs. Smith at 9:30 and Mr. Bengston at 10:15."

"Ugh, I have Marvin at 10:30," said Mark, looking at his clipboard.

"I'll take Marvin," I said. "You can have Mr. Bengston."

"You did get lucky!" Angela said emphatically to the laughter of my co-workers.

"Nope. I'm just trying to be in a good mood," I replied again.

Later that morning, I met Marvin at the elevator. His cane was in one hand, a plastic bag in the other. I helped him walk to the examining room where I would treat him.

Marvin stopped at Angela's desk where the bagels were arranged neatly on a plastic tray. "Yum, bagels," he said, and grabbed two of them. He placed one in each of his coat pockets.

"OK, Marvin, I'm going to need to you lie down on the table," I said as we entered the room.

"You got it, Jane." He said and slowly lowered his back onto the table. I was rather shocked by his compliance.

"OK, I'm just going to raise your legs one at a time."
I picked up his left leg.

"Ouch!"

"Did I hurt you?"

"Nah, it's Ok." Marvin looked at me with a smile.

"You seem happy today," I said.

"I am," he replied. "I want to show you something."

"What?" I said.

"Look in the bag."

"One second." I set his leg down on the bed and
walked to the plastic take-out bag he had placed on a
chair. I opened it. I couldn't believe what I saw.

"You said knitting would help me relax. I'm giving
it a go."

"Marvin, this is incredible!" I pulled a neatly wound
ball of New York Yankees navy blue wool and two
wooden knitting needles from the bag.

"I'm making a scarf," he said. "I'm gonna wear it at
my Yankees bar. It's my wife's old yarn."

"Your pals will all be jealous."

"They already are."

"How did you learn how to do this?"

"I was married for twenty years – I learned a lot of things from her." He added, "Besides, I think it helps my hands."

"You just made my day!" I said. "And, I have a surprise for you, too. Hold on."

I rushed out of the room and into the reception area. I kept my personal items behind Angela's desk. I rummaged through my purse.

"These are for you," I said, re-entering the room. I held up the finished Koigu socks. "I hope you like them."

"You made these?" he asked. He reached down and started yanking off his old, stained, white athletic socks. "They're gorgeous, darlin."

"Just for you," I said. "Finished them this morning."

Finally freeing his foot from the soggy sock, he took a sock I had knitted him and slid it over his toes and up his shin. He lifted his own leg in front of him to admire the sock, wiggling his toes. "My, my, Jane, they're great!" he said.

"It's my pleasure, Marvin. No, no – sit down!" But Marvin was already struggling to dismount the table, white paper sheet a-rustling beneath his gouty leg. "Marvin!"

With a final "Umph!" he hoisted himself up and levered himself off the table. He hobbled toward me and wrapped me in a big, heavy hug.

"Aww. Marvin," I said. "You're very welcome."

"My wife was a big knitter," Marvin said, ambling back toward the table. "She used to knit something every month or so. I've still got some of the things she made for me. Though I wish I had worn them more, or cared more about them when she was alive. But I'll take good care of these, Jane." He indicated the socks. "I'll wear them till they fall off my feet." I grabbed his arm and helped him get back on the table.

When the session ended I walked him arm-in-arm through the reception room. Marvin stopped once again at Angela's desk.

"Only one bagel left. Don't mind if I do," he said grabbing it and stuffing it in his bagel-filled jacket pockets.

I could hear Mark's voice from behind me. "Dammit," he said under his breath, eyes on the crumb-filled tray. I just laughed as I helped Marvin into the elevator.

It was one of the best days I had at work in a while. After Marvin, the rest of the day breezed by quickly.

On the way home, I decided to keep knitting while waiting for the PATH train to pick me up. Standing up, I began casting-on the lace-weight yarn for the cowl onto a pair of size 6, 24-inch metal circular needles. Yarn unwound from a skein in my purse.

I began counting to myself…34, 35, 36, 37…

Standing next to me was a guy in a dark suit. *Is he looking at me?* I lost count of my cast-on stitches and looked up to see him leaning against the next pole. He was reading *The Wall Street Journal* when I caught his eyes peeking over the paper. I tried to re-focus on my knitting, but my stomach began to flutter. He was tall with brown hair and had a brushed wool overcoat folded over one arm. When I caught his eyes again, he quickly turned his glance away.

The train pulled into the 14th Street station and the doors opened. I placed my needles in my bag and waited for passengers to exit. The train was going to be crowded. A couple standing just inside the door squeezed past me and I stepped into the first car. The guy came in right behind me. I saw two seats straight ahead. I took one. The guy took the other.

"HO - bo – ken train!" exclaimed the conductor. I took out my knitting again. I started to count, again, how many stitches were on my needles. I was losing track over and over. Our shoulders just ever-so-lightly brushed as the train lurched forward. I tried not to look at him though I could tell he was looking at me.

"What are you knitting?" he asked.

He didn't say, "I didn't know girls still knit," or, "my mother knits," or, worst of all, "are you crocheting?" *Crochet doesn't use needles! It uses hooks!* Instead, he asked, "What are you knitting?" It was a good sign.

"A cowl," I said. "I just started."

I turned my head slightly and saw his blue eyes. I smiled and bashfully went back to casting on.

"Do you live in Hoboken?" he asked.

"Yes," I said, "I just moved in. Do you?"

"I used to. I live in the city now. I'm meeting friends tonight at Galligan's. Have you been there?"

"Not yet."

"I'm Andrew," he said.

"Jane," I responded. "Nice to meet you." I smiled and pretended to keep counting stitches.

"Galligan's is on First Street, if you want to drop by."

"Not tonight," I said.

"Then another night. Can I call you?"

I paused, my stomach fluttering. *Oh my god he's asking me out.* I looked up into his eyes. His gaze was piercing, staring right into me. His blue eyes were beautiful. I could barely take my eyes away. *Yes! Yes!* I was saying to myself. *Yes you can call me!*

But instead, I said, "Do you always pick up girls on the subway?"

He looked pretty embarrassed. He turned away.

Ah! What was that? Out of the corner of my eye I saw him grimace. He was staring very intently, it seemed, in the direction exactly opposite to me.

Idiot! My mind raced for something to say. "I'm so sorry. I'm just kidding. That was nice of you to invite me."

He turned back to me. "No, it's ok."

"I hear the Subway's a great place to pick up girls."

"I've actually never picked anyone up on the subway, so. And I guess I won't try it again."

I noticed an older woman across the aisle watching us as if we were an old movie. I reached into my purse, wrote my cell number on the back of a business card. I clutched it in my hand. The train began to slow, the brakes began to screech; we were nearing the end.

I held my hand out to him. "Here."

He looked up at me. He waited a second – as if to say, *are you for real?* – and took the card. When he saw what I had written on it, he smiled.

"HO – bo – ken," interrupted the conductor.

MARVIN'S SOCKS
Pattern by David Klueger

Marvin's Socks

PATRICIA AND ADAM SCRIBNER

A great pair of socks made out of gorgeous yarn. David wrote this pattern with the experienced knitter in mind. For abbreviations, please see list at end of book.

Yarn: Koigu KPPPM 2 hanks main color (mc), 1 hank contrasting color(cc)

Needles: US 4 Double pointed needles (dpn's)

Gauge: 7sts = 1 inch on US 4's

Cuff

CO 58 stitches with CC

Join in the rnd being careful not to twist stitches.

Work K1, P1 rib for 2 inches.

Calf

Switch to MC

K 1 rd, decreasing 1 st somewhere in the rd, ending with the total of 57 sts. Work in St. st. for 5 ½ inches.

Ankle

Knit one rnd increasing 9 sts evenly . 66 sts.

Knit even for 1 inch

Heel

Divide sts evenly on 2 needles (33 per)

K 33 sts, turn and P 33 sts.

Repeat previous step until flap is 2 ¼ inches

Turn Heel

1. K 20, K2tog, K1, turn
2. Sl 1, P8, P2tog, P1, Turn
3. Sl 1, K9, K2tog, K1, Turn
4. Sl 1, P10, P2tog, P1, Turn
5. Sl 1, K11, K2tog, K1, Turn
6. Sl 1, P12, P2tog, P1, Turn
7. Sl 1, K13, K2tog, K1, Turn

8. Sl 1, P14, P2tog, P1, Turn
9. Sl 1, K15, K2tog, K1, Turn
10. Sl 1, P16, P2tog, P1, Turn
11. Sl 1, K17, K2tog, K1, Turn
12. Sl 1, P18, P2tog, P1, Turn
13. K across

There should be 21 sts remaining for heel.

Instep

PU and K 13 sts, k across instep (33 sts), PU and K 13 sts on other side of heel, K11

Divide the sts over 3 DPNs.

1st needle- 23 sts (gusset and heel)

2nd needle- 33 sts (instep)

3rd needle- 24 sts (gusset)

1st Round: K around

2nd Round: 1st needle: K to last 3 sts, K2tog, K 1

2nd needle: K across

3rd needle: K 1, SSK, K to the end of the needle

Repeat 1st and 2nd rnds until 66 sts remain (16, 33, 17)

Gusset: K around for 3 inches

Toe

Change to CC

1st Round: K around

2nd Round: 1st needle: K to last 3 sts, K2tog, K 1

2nd needle: K across

3rd needle: K 1, SSK, K to the end of the needle

Repeat 1st and 2nd rnds until 34 sts remain

Divide the sts evenly on two DPNs (17 each)

Kitchner Stitch the toe closed.
Break yarn, weave in ends, Bob's your uncle.

Chapter 11: Opening Up

The next evening I dropped by Patricia's Yarns to sign up for the next knit night on Friday. Patricia was teaching a private lesson to two children.

I waited until she had the two children purling before I said, "I had so much fun at knit night last week. Is there still room for this week?"

"For you? Of course!" She got up and went to her counter. "Jane…what is your last name?" she asked, opening a folder lying on the countertop.

"Sullivan," I responded. "How many people do you have at knit night?"

"Eight," she said, jotting my name down. "But last week we made an exception for you," she said, smiling at the book as she wrote in it.

I gave Patricia five dollars to hold my spot. "It's for wine and snacks," she said.

"I have a lot to talk about this week," I said.

"I look forward to hearing it. Margaux has a pretty good story as well. She told it to me last night and I couldn't stop laughing."

Michelle opened the shop door carrying two coffees in a tray. "Hey Jane," she said walking to the table.

"Skim latte," she announced in Patricia's direction and placed the coffee on the table. "And this is for Riley." Riley ran from the back of the shop. "Sit, Ri!" Michelle was waving the cardboard coffee tray over the little dog's head. Riley sat on his hind legs. A tiny tooth poked out from his mouth as he waited patiently. Michelle handed him the tray. He snatched it from her hand, shook his head from side to side with a growl, and ran back to his bed in the back of the shop to chew on it.

One of the two little girls having a lesson spoke up, "Aww, he's so cute!"

Michelle pulled up a chair and started knitting. Patricia sat back down with the kids. I started to walk to the door. "I'll see you guys soon," I said, halfway out the door, a hand up in farewell.

"Wait? You're leaving?" asked Michelle.

"Yes. I need a quiet night at home. I'll see you at knit night on Friday, though."

"Oh good," said Michelle. "I'll see you then."

***

After two morning physical therapy sessions, Mark and I went for a walk out on 6th Avenue to get lunch. "I'm buying," he insisted with a laugh as we walked to the hot dog vendor on the corner. In true New

York City fashion, we ordered two dirty-water dogs and two Cokes.

"Ooh," I teased. "Do you take all the girls here?"

"Only pretty ones," he said.

I looked up to Mark. He had been at the office five years before I came on. He was a very respected physical therapist, and I always liked the way he interacted with his patients. He's, what I would describe as, "a good guy".

"You seem to be doing all right this week." He said and took a big bite of hot dog. "I was worried about you last week," he continued with his mouth half-full, licking mustard off his lip.

"I'm doing all right," I responded. "Last week was obviously tough."

"Have you heard from Dennis?" he asked.

"No. Just a stupid note attached to my necklace he sent over. He said I could call him. But he has yet to pick up the phone and call me."

"You sure?"

"No messages. No missed calls. Haven't talked to him since that first day I caught him cheating."

"Tell me again how that happened?"
Knowing that I still had at least an hour before my next patient, I began telling him about the sweater and the morning I saw it on another girl.

"And do you know what the craziest thing is? I gave it to him only two days before."

"What's crazy about that?" he asked.

"It may seem weird, but knitters have a theory. If you knit your boyfriend a sweater, they'll break up with you." I looked at Mark with my eyebrows raised. I was waiting to see if he thought I was nuts. "It's called the Curse of the Boyfriend Sweater."

I expected Mark to laugh, but he didn't.

"Makes sense," he said, still chewing. "You spend all that time working on something for someone – it's a big commitment. It's like a hand-made engagement ring. I can see how that could cause a break-up, scare a guy away."

"But we had been together for *three years*, Mark. I lived with the guy."

He shrugged and kept chewing.

"Would you be scared away?" I asked.

"Depends on who makes me the sweater," he said. "What that doesn't explain, though, is how come he had planned this whole Seattle ruse out ahead of time. You thought he was going to Seattle way before you gave him the sweater. But he never was going to Seattle. It was just some kind of a scheme to cheat on you or something."

"I know, Mark, I know! I think he knew I was knitting it, though."

"Did Dennis cheat on you before?"

My guess was yes. I shook my head up and down.

"I'm really sorry, Jane—"

But my cell phone ring interrupted. I didn't recognize the number.

"Oh god!" I said to Mark. "This could be the new guy I met."

"New Guy? Already?" Mark said, looking at me awkwardly. "You move on quickly," he whispered and turned his back as I picked up the call.

My stomach fluttered. "Hello?" I said into the phone.

"Is this Jane?" asked the voice on the other end of the line.

"Yes," I said. My voice cracked. "Who's this?"

"I'm Andrew. Remember me from the PATH train?" I paused, trying to play it cool, making it seem like I was trying to remember. "Uhhh. Oh, yeah. Sure. Hi."

I pushed the phone against my cheek to hear him better over the city traffic. There was a pause. It was a long pause. "Hello?" I said again…nothing.

I looked at my phone. "Crap," I said.

Mark turned toward me. "What?" he asked.

"I think I just hung up on him. Damn!"

Mark started to laugh. I hit him with the flat of my hand against his chest. "Dammit, I hate this phone."

"Ouch," said Mark. "Take it easy."

It rang again. I took a deep breath and motioned with my finger to my lips for Mark to be quiet.

"Jane? You there?" asked Andrew.

"Yes, sorry. My phone sucks." *Did I just say 'sucks'?*

"I'm calling to see if you're available for dinner Saturday," he said.

Yes! Yes, I am! "I am," I said as calmly as possible. *Ooh, he was so formal about it.*

"Great. I'll come to Hoboken. Let's say 8pm, at Elysian Café."

I didn't know the place, but, "sounds great. See you then!" I said.

"Oh, and Jane."

"Yeah?"

"It's a first."

"What is?"

"Good-bye, Jane."

I snapped my phone closed and with a little happy smile said "Yay!" I caught Mark by surprise and gave him a big hug.

"I guess that was the new guy," he said.

"Yup," I said excitedly.

I texted Rachel: "Guess what?" And without waiting for a response, I texted again "I have a date on Sat!"

Knit night was Friday and my big date with Andrew was Saturday. I couldn't wait for the weekend!

***

Friday, I decided to leave work early and go straight to Patricia's. When I got there, Patricia was behind the counter looking through catalogs. Along with Heather and Jamison, a girl I hadn't met before was sitting at the round table.

"Hi Jane," said Patricia. "How's your cowl coming along?"

"Not too quickly," I replied. "My size-sixes are definitely slowing me down!"

"Size-six needles slow everyone down," said Patricia. "Hey, Jane, do you know Mia?" Patricia pointed to the petite, dark-haired girl sitting on the opposite side of the table. She looked young enough to be carded at any bar. "Mia is working on a cowl too."

"Nice to meet you, Jane," Mia said.

Mia lifted a gorgeous fingering-weight yarn, also in grayscale tones. The pattern of the cowl looked like seashells.

"Ooh, beautiful cowl," I said. "I'm making a cowl right now, too, for my mother."

"Oh, yeah, I just made one for my mother," Mia said.

"This one's for me, though. I want to wear it with a new cocktail dress I bought."

"How long have you been knitting?" I asked.

"Two years."

"But Mia doesn't stop knitting," interrupted Patricia. "She is one of our best knitters."

"Patricia taught me," Mia said.

"*And so young.*" Patricia said with her best grandmother accent. "She is a very quick learner."

The shop door opened.

"What's up ladies?" Margaux came swaggering in. "I'm running for coffee. Does anyone want one? Thought I'd have a latte before I have some wine," she said, laughing.

"I'll take one," said Patricia.

"Does she always have that much energy?" I asked Patricia as Margaux ran out the door.

"No, usually, she has more," she replied.

I pulled a little brown chair from the corner to the table and sat down. Just as my bottom was about to hit chair, Mia and Patricia both exclaimed simultaneously: "Wait!" I froze, eyes wide, looking at them.

"What?" I asked.

Mia laughed. Patricia said, "That chair's a little rickety. Nobody can sit in it except for Riley and Michelle."

"Riley, because he's a tiny dog and weighs about six pounds," Mia said, "and Michelle, because she's a ballerina. She sits amazingly still. If any of us sat in it," she looked from me to Patricia, "it would fall to pieces."

Trish added, "Margaux found that out the hard way! The truth is, it was my parents' chair. It's an antique. I should get rid of it, but I can't."

I carefully replaced the chair in its spot in the corner, and put a basket of yarn on it as warning to the next unsuspecting passer-by. I grabbed another chair and sat next to Mia. I took out my knitting. "What do you do, Mia?" I asked.

"I'm a student," she said. "And you?"

I told her I was a physical therapist, but didn't get much farther than that before people started streaming into the shop. First was David.

"I brought some beer," he said and yanked a six-pack of Bear Bier out of his oversized messenger bag. "This stuff is my favorite."

"Oh my god," said Mia. "Bear Bier has the dumbest advertisements."

"What?! They're so good. With the bears drinking beers with the Vikings in the Lower East Side. Those bears are so cool." He put on the trademark Bear accent, "Bier. Bär Bier. Beer for Bears.' It's so funny how they capitalize on the linguistic similarity between 'bear' and 'beer' in English and Dutch. Or is it German?"

"My ex-boyfriend was an executive at the company that made those commercials," I said.

David and Mia turned to me. It was the first time, I think, that I had talked about Dennis to anyone that hadn't known him before we broke up.

"Cool," said David. "Did you get lots of free Bear Bier from him?"

"You know it's made by Coors, right?" I said.

"Really? I thought it was imported from Iceland?" David looked perturbed. "Or at least Canada."

He spun the six-pack around and inspected the back. "Oh yeah," he said. "Distributed by Coors Brewing

Company, Golden, Colorado. Brewed in Kearny, NJ. Damn."

"Dennis wrote some of the original copy on those ads two years ago."

"I remember the first commercial came out in the '07 Super Bowl. The bears all getting loaded and playing football on the tundra. Ha. It was hilarious. Of course, the Bears didn't win that Super Bowl."

"Dennis was from Chicago," I said.

"I thought they were stupid – no offense, Jane," said Mia.

"None taken," I replied.

"They weren't going for you," said David. "They were going for me. Large, whiskered, late-twenties male, with a possible bear somewhere far back on their evolutionary tree. You're not their target group."

But the debate on Bear Bier's advertising targets was interrupted when the door swung open and Margaux walked in with Michelle. "Look who I ran into on the way!" said Margaux. She passed a couple of cups of coffee around.

"Hey everyone." Michelle was carrying a bottle of wine and a grocery bag. "Trish, I found the cheese and crackers, but couldn't find the wine we had last week."

"Not a problem," said Patricia. "I don't think this group is too choosy."

"I did get *these*, though…" said Michelle. She reached into the bag and pulled out a large container of chocolate-covered pretzels. Patricia snatched them and put them in her purse.

"Oh, no you don't," said Margaux, grabbing for the pretzels. She undid the lid and took a couple. "So," she said, munching, "I have a good story to tell."

"I heard," I said. "I've been looking forward to it."

"So, we were at a bar in New York last weekend," Margaux started. "Jamison, Michelle, and I were all there drinking, dancing, you know, just having fun."

"And there was a bachelor party going on," interrupted Jamison.

"We had a few glasses of wine and started dancing with the guys. They started buying us drinks. It seemed harmless," Margaux continued.

"The bachelor was wearing a white t-shirt and his friends were handing out markers and telling girls to write things on his shirt," said Jamison.

"So on the way back from the bathroom," Margaux said, "I grabbed a marker from the hostess' table. At that point, people had already written quite a few things on him. The shirt was filling up. People wrote 'I love you!' or 'don't do it!' They drew breasts on it. You know, the usual stupid bachelor party stuff."
"Did I mention that this bachelor had already hit on me – drunk- a few times," said Michelle loudly.

"No, but that is important to the story," said Margaux emphatically. "Because Michelle, after another glass of wine, takes my marker, walks up to the poor guy, who, at this point, had way too much in him already and, after looking for a place to write on his shirt, instead chooses to write 'YEAH BABY'… on his forehead!"

"Oops," said Michelle sheepishly.

"The worst part was Michelle woke up in the morning and had the marker in her bag. And… I'll let Michelle tell the rest of the story," said Margaux.

"It was a permanent marker," said Michelle.

"The guy was getting married the next day!" said Margaux.

"I *really* didn't know it was permanent," said Michelle, shaking her head, covering her mouth.

"Oh my god," I said loudly over the laughter of the room. "Poor guy."

There was a rapping at the door. It was Anna. She tapped a bottle of wine on the glass.

"Anna!" exclaimed Margaux.
"She has wine, let her in!" cried Heather.

Patricia got up and opened the door.

"Room for one mo'?" asked Anna in her New Zealand accent.

"For you, of course," said Patricia.

"Did I miss anything?" asked Anna.

"Yeah baby," said Michelle to a chorus of laughter.

"I'll fill you in later," said a giggling Patricia to Anna.

Margaux, still holding the group's attention, said, "so, Jane, tell us more about you."

Last week, I didn't really open up to the others. But this week was different. "Well, I just moved to Hoboken, as you know. I had been living in Tribeca for three years—"

"Ooh fancy," said Margaux.

"—but had to leave when my boyfriend and I broke up."

"Ooh, that's sad," said Margaux.

"Or, I *guess* he broke up with me. I suppose I was going to break up with him, because I found out that he had been cheating on me. But, I'm actually not sure if I would have."

"I would have dumped him right on the *spot*," said Margaux.

"Was this the first time he cheated on you?" asked Mia.

"No, I don't think it was the first time," I replied. "I have no real way of knowing, of course, but Dennis – my ex – I think lied about a lot of things. When we were breaking up over the phone, he implied that he's lied to me about this before."

"And you weren't going to dump him?" asked Margaux.

"Well...I don't know. I mean obviously this spells the end of our relationship. But it would have been hard for me to do that. Dennis provided me with a lot of things."

Trish asked, "How did you finally figure it out?"

CURSE OF THE BOYFRIEND SWEATER

Margaux said, "Intuition. You can usually figure these things out after a while. Right? The stories just don't match up." She looked in my direction for confirmation.

"Actually," I said, "it was because of something I had knitted for him."

"What do you mean?" asked Michelle.

"Have you girls ever heard of the Curse of the Boyfriend Sweater?"

A palpable shiver could be felt by everyone in the room. Mia dropped her needles to the floor. In the silence that descended, the sound rang out throughout the shop. Margaux swilled a glass of wine. Trish's knitting speed slowed threefold. All gazes went towards me.

"I knew that was a real thing," whispered Michelle.

"I knit Dennis a sweater," I said. "It was amazing. I spent about three months on it. And I'm not a slow knitter. Dennis wasn't home much, so I had time to work on it when I was alone, in the apartment. It was a dark blue Merino wool V-neck done in a seed stitch. I tailored the sweater just for him, taking secret measurements when he wasn't looking. Every measurement was custom-fit: each sleeve, the taper of the trunk, the width of the shoulders. I worked in a nice, soft neckband so it wouldn't scratch his shaven neck. Dennis always complained about razor burn. I spent all my spare time on that sweater, sneaking in hours when Dennis wasn't around, to make sure it was a surprise for him."

"And so what happened?" Mia asked, wide-eyed.

All the girls had stopped knitting, and were leaning in toward me. Even David had abandoned his beer and looked entranced.

"I think he hated it."

"No!" shouted Margaux.

"How could he?!" shrieked Mia.

"Well, I'll never know, will I?" I said. "All I know, is that two days later, I'm walking in Manhattan and I see a model-type brunette stalking up the avenue wearing *the* sweater. I wouldn't mistake that sweater anywhere. "

"Oh. My. God," said Michelle.

I continued, "I called Dennis, and he flat-out told me he was cheating on me. And, I'm assuming he hasn't gotten the sweater back and that's the last I've heard from him."

There was a long pause. No one spoke.

"Oh my god," echoed Mia.

"That's awful," said Margaux.

"I'm not knitting a boyfriend sweater until there is a ring on this finger," said Michelle, holding up her hand. "And even then, who knows."

"But," I said, "to try and make this story have a fairy tale ending, I did just meet a new guy…"

"Ooooh," said Mia.

"Where did you meet him?" Michelle asked.

"On the PATH," I replied.

"On the *PATH*?" Margaux laughed. "Uh oh. What kind of a guy is this?"

"Don't worry," I assured her. "He's not homeless. I think."

"I hope not."

"That's hot," said Mia. "I always wondered what it would be like to meet a guy on the subway."

"I have a date tomorrow," I said.

"Oh, you *have* to tell us how it goes," Patricia said.

"I will," I said, smiling. "I promise."

Chapter 12: First Date

Saturday morning. I looked at the cowl I had been knitting. *Oh crap.* I would have to rip back at least ten rows. Such is the standard knitter's hangover. I dimly remembered, amid the laughter of the night before, someone joking that knitting only gets harder the more you drink red wine. I had to concur.

But, I had a big date coming up, and there were things to do, plans to be made, and, of course, outfits to choose.

"Shopping?" I texted to Rachel.

"NYC not Hob," she texted back immediately.

That afternoon, I hopped on the PATH train to 9th Street in New York City and walked through the NYU Campus to meet Rachel in SOHO.

"I need something that is going to make me look great," I said to her at the corner of Prince and Broadway.

"Not a problem," she replied. "But first, we need manicures"

We walked to the edge of Chinatown and dipped into a little place that had a sign that said "day spa." *This is a day spa?* It was the size of my kitchen.

CURSE OF THE BOYFRIEND SWEATER

"Are you sure this place is good?" I asked Rachel.

"Trust me, I always come here," she said. "This place is the best."

I had to bend my neck as to not bump my head on the way down the stairs to the salon. I was guided to and sat down in an old leather chair. Fumes of nail polish remover were thick in the stale air. *Isn't there a window in this place?* An older Asian woman, wearing a surgical mask, without saying a word, grabbed my hand and began a soft message. As she pushed on the soft spot between my thumb and pointer finger, I closed my eyes. In seemingly minutes, our fingers were painted and dried a bright red.

We strolled down the cobblestone streets of SOHO, stopping at the various windows of boutiques along the way. For winter, it was rather nice outside, though there was a strong wind gusting about. Street debris would swirl in little cyclones as we walked. I had to clasp my hat to hold it on my head.

I stopped dead in my tracks in front of a shop display window. "That's the dress," I said to Rachel, pointing at a black Diane von Furstenburg. "That is definitely the dress." It had a long swooping neckline, a belt, and a slit up the thigh. I took Rachel by the hand and entered the shop.

I picked it up and felt it. It felt sensational against my arm, my cheek.. It was perfect. I had to try it on. I checked the price tag. *Oh, god!* It cost a month in rent.

"It will look great with my Fendi handbag," Rachel said encouragingly with a wink.

"See, I'm saving money already," I joked. "If I buy this, can I borrow your Fendi tonight?"

"Absolutely," she said. "You're going to look stunning!"

***

By the time I got home, showered, and put on make-up, I only had minutes to make it to Elysian Café in time to meet Andrew.

"Wow," he said, already standing at the bar when I arrived in the black dress. "You look amazing."

"Thanks," I said, blushing. "You look great too." He was wearing a dark sport coat and a deep blue shirt that complimented his eyes. Andrew had a total baby-face, though a good shave line was visible, and it made it hard to tell how old he was. He could have been right out of college, or in his mid-thirties.

"What can I get you?" he asked.

"Vodka and soda," I said.

He ordered a scotch and water.

"How was your trip here?" I asked.

"Good. I miss this commute, actually. Hoboken is closer to a lot of my clients than where I live in the city."

He handed me my drink and said, "Cheers."

"Cheers to what?" I asked.

"Umm. Cheers…to…"

"We have to toast something."

"Cheers to…here's to a good night."

"Good night!" I feigned walking to the door. "Haha – just kidding!" *Why do I have to be so weird?*

"Good one, Jane," he said.

Whew!

"To Lancelot," he said.

"What?" I was confused.

"A good knight."

Ah. "Arguably." I wracked my brain for Camelot references.

"True," he rejoined. "Code of Chivalry a little tested with Guenevere and all that."

I smiled. "Cheers to a good night," and we clinked glasses.

We were seated at a marble-top table. The waiters wore dress shirts and ties and had an air of formality to them, but the atmosphere was comfortable. The décor was 19th Century Parisian. We sipped our cocktails.

"So," I said. "Am I *really* the first girl you've ever hit-on on the subway?

"Hit-on or picked up?"

"Oh! There's a difference?"

"Sure," he said, smiling. "One implies success and the other a lack of it."

"So...?"

"Well, yeah, all the time," he joked. "Every day, a new subway girlfriend."

"Wait, really?"

"Of course. They call me the subway Casanova. Because of how I seduce beautiful young females on the PATH train. Steal their hearts, that is. I'm infamous. I'm surprised you haven't heard of me. Swooning women littering 33rd Street."

"Gross."

"Well, you know, not littering, just swooning, perhaps. "

"Alone with their memories?"

"Like shells. Zombies."

"And where their hearts used to be, only the fleeting image of you. *Andrew*."

"Powerful. I am."

"So that's why all the stone-dead-looking people at 8 a.m. on the PATH train."

He laughed. "No, I think that's just because they haven't had their coffee yet."

"Coffee can't replace their hearts. Or make up for you," I smiled.

"I think for some it can," he said.

"Yes, I need my coffee." I laughed.

He smiled. "No, you're *really* the first."

"First victim?" I asked, genuinely curious.

He feigned a – 'No, you know what I mean' look, then smiled, "Yes. First victim. Watch out."

"How do you know this isn't what I always do too?"

"Oh yes. I was warned about you. The knitting killer."

"The knitting killer?"

"A beautiful, charming, innocent-looking girl knitting a cowl on the PATH platform. Lovely gray-blue eyes. Just crying out to be hit on. The scourge of Hoboken males. Hearts throbbing all the way down Washington Street. Using your knitting needles like twin daggers, isolating dapper young businessmen with wool coats to expunge. Exterminate. Eliminate."

"Wait I thought we were talking metaphorically? Like not actually killing, but like slaying meaning the hearts of."

"We were. And, literally. You might be both. Hearts then minds, right? Hearts then bodies?"

"Hearts then minds, that's me" I said with a smile.

"I knew it."

"You're pretty good with words, Andrew," I said.

"In advertising, you have to be good with words," he replied. "To sell products. You know, clever phrases and everything."

"So you work in advertising?" *God, I really do have a type.*

"Yes I do."

"So tell me something about yourself. Like, where are you from?" I asked.

"Seattle."

"You're a long way from home, Andrew. Do you miss it?"

"Sometimes. I love New York, though. How about you?"

"I'm a Jersey girl," I said proudly.

"Of course, you are. Do Jersey girls ever leave New Jersey?"

"Only temporarily," I said.

"I knew it," he said, smiling.

 "Come, on, tell me something I should know about you? Something you wouldn't normally tell on a first date."

He looked at me and smiled. "Hmm, well. No. I thought this wasn't going to come out until dessert, but…I don't like chocolate."

"Gasp." *What?* "Wait…really? Isn't that like criminal? I don't think you can become a citizen in Australia with those credentials. I'm pretty sure the U.S. has laws about that too."

"Yes, they do. I'm wanted in fourteen states," he said.

"I've actually heard it posited by the more biologically inclined friends of mine that there is actually a gender divide on the subject of chocolate-liking-inclinations."

"I have never dated a man who hasn't liked chocolate."

"Maybe he's just never told you."

"I mean, yay, maybe, but… I would kill for a really, really good piece of dark chocolate."

"But that's just because you're sadistic. Not necessarily proof of my thesis."

"I think most girls I know would too," I said.

"Well," said Andrew taking a deep breath and picking up his menu. "Fortunately, there are many things on this menu that don't involve chocolate that I'm sure we both can agree on."

I picked up the menu. "Mmm, the short ribs sound good," I said.

The waiter came over. "Have you decided on dinner?"

Andrew looked at me. "Are you ready?"

I shook my head yes and mouthed "short ribs."

"Yes. I am going to have the shrimp for an appetizer and the rosemary brined pork chop and Jane is going to have the Burgundy braised beef short ribs."

"Very good," the waiter said.

I smiled at Andrew.

The night went on like that. We talked like we had known each other for years. He was so cute and flirty and such a gentleman. Turns out he went to Fordham. He had only graduated a couple years ahead of me.

After dinner, we walked down town to the Hoboken PATH station. We hovered outside the steps leading down to the platform. It was a cool night and I shivered a bit. "I had a great time," I said.

"Me too," he said and leaned closer.

I bit my lower lip in anticipation. He gave me a kiss on the cheek. He said again, "I had a great time tonight," his face half an inch away from mine.

"Me too," I whispered back.

He kissed me on the lips and said, "I had a great time tonight."

"Andrew," I laughed, "how was your evening?"

He turned mock serious. "It was very good. In fact, if I had to categorize the time I had this evening, I would say 'I had a great time tonight.'" I smiled.

"Good night, Jane."

"Good night."

After Andrew got on the train, I was glowing. I basked in the moonlight and floated the seven blocks back to my apartment. I walked upstairs and let the door close behind me. I stood with my back to it for several minutes, just smiling.

CURSE OF THE BOYFRIEND SWEATER

***

The next morning, my phone rang.

"Hi Janie."

"Dad! How are you?"

"I'm ok."

"*Where* are you?"

"I'm still living at the hotel. Do you have a moment? I want to talk to you."

"Of course, Dad."

My Dad normally doesn't say much when it comes to his personal life. Today, he opened up. He told me that money was tight, since he was paying about $60 a night for his tiny single at the Best Western in Secaucus.

I passed that hotel a thousand times going home on breaks to New Jersey, seeing the big logo reflection in the river below from my vantage point on the NJ Transit train car. I never in a million years thought my father would be living there.

My dad said he had been going back and forth to work daily from the hotel, that he had moved his favorite reading chair from his study into the corner of the hotel room, and had brought a whole milk crate of books from the house.

"I don't get too many visitors out here."

"Oh, Dad."

"No, no, it's ok," he said. "As the great Paul Simon once wrote, *'I've got my books and my poetry to protect me.'*"

"Why don't you just go home and be with Mom?" I finally asked.

"I can't," he replied. "But it's going to be ok. I'm looking for my own place."

"Do you want me to visit?"

"I would love a visit from you . But hopefully I'll have a new apartment soon, and you can visit me there."

"Why can't you go home?"

"I'm sorry, honey, but that is between me and you're your mother. Soon enough, you'll understand. You will."

Chapter 13: Flowers Bloom in Hoboken

By the time Hoboken was ready to host its annual Spring Arts and Music Festival, the problems of winter seemed of a distant past.

Cherry blossoms were in full bloom on First Street and tulips were planted in the street-side garden that ran the length of Eleventh. There were pots full of pansies, daffodils, and dahlias all along the city's walkways and stoops. Hoboken girls traded their long, dark coats for short, brightly patterned skirts. Boys were wearing short sleeves. Children chalked their names onto sidewalks and rode around on scooters and bicycles. People sat and had drinks at outdoor cafes. Large, colorful umbrellas hovered over tables and welcomed people to the numerous restaurants that lined Washington Street. Even Patricia held one-on-one knitting lessons outside at a small table in front of her shop.

Although my parents hadn't officially divorced, they had separated and divided their belongings. My father found a modest apartment in Jersey City and was, in his words, finally able to get out and play golf. My mother was visiting me weekly and finding companionship in her Mahjong group at her church. Andrew and I were doing great. We had gone on four dates (not that I was counting) and we started to talk more regularly on the phone. I wasn't ready to get serious with a guy again, but loved having someone to go out with on weekends.

PATRICIA AND ADAM SCRIBNER

Through the knit shop, I had made many new friends in Hoboken. I continuously ran into them on the streets and in restaurants. Instead of a city, Hoboken was beginning to feel like a neighborhood. Those anonymous windows from my first few nights started revealing people behind them. Even Rachel was enjoying her visits to see me, and making more trips to "the Boken."

And I finished the cowl for Mom, just in time for Mother's Day.

I needed a new project, so I stopped by Patricia's on a sunny Friday afternoon. I left the office early, so I had the whole afternoon stretching out before me. Trish was sitting out front knitting. Leashed at her feet sat Riley, watching closely as pedestrians walked by. Next to her was a man I hadn't met before.

"Jane, this is Chris," she said, introducing him.

"Nice to meet you," I said. *A second male knitter shouldn't be too hard to remember.*

Chris was cute. He was dressed trendily in a pair of skinny jeans and a patterned shirt. His hair was perfectly parted. He had a tattoo of words running the length of his right arm, though I'm not sure what they said. His soft face told me he was just out of college. Despite the warm weather, he was knitting a wool sweater.

CURSE OF THE BOYFRIEND SWEATER

"Nice sweater, Chris," I said.

"Thanks. It's based on an Elizabeth Zimmerman pattern."

"Ooh, cool."

"Yeah, I like the way she writes patterns. I can customize what she writes and work on something that's fit for me." He held up the sweater to his arm to eyeball a measurement. "Ah, shoot."

"What's wrong?"

"Well," he said, undoing a row of stitches. "Sometimes it takes ripping out and re-doing...but the end product is worth it. What do you think?"

"Yeah, it looks great. And I love the hood."

"I'm thinking perfect for late nights out in fall," he said looking up at me.

"You're getting me excited. Trish, I need a new project," I exclaimed.

"Something for Andrew?" she asked, inflecting her voice.

"Oh no! Not a boyfriend project. I just want something new and different – something unique. What are you making?" I asked her.

"A sweater for Riley." She held up a tiny dog sweater. Riley heard his name and looked up from the ground.

"Go on inside and take a look around," said Patricia. "See if anything catches your eye. Holler if you need me." She went back to clicking her needles.

I walked into the shop and started touching all of the beautiful yarns. Patricia had changed her displays for spring. There were new little girls' dresses and tiny baby booties hung from string, like a cute little clothesline, in the window. There was a robin's egg blue sweater fit on the mannequin, and, draped over the ballerina's chair, a multi-colored mitered square blanket. It was beautiful, and seemed to shimmer and refract light right there on the chair's back.

"Tell me about this blanket. I love it." I said, lifting it off the chair back and carrying it to the door.

Patricia came inside. "I made that blanket two years ago. It uses a pattern that was created by a few of us here at the shop for the Hoboken Homeless Shelter Auction. I liked it so much, I made another for myself." She pointed me toward a large display of Koigu Yarn, the same yarn I used to make Marvin's socks.

There were dusty earth tones and brilliant jewel tones - and those were just the solid-colored options. Patricia reached into a cubby and pulled out a multi-colored skein. The colors bled from one into another, from deep blues to purples to browns to golds.

"The best part about a project like this is that you don't have to buy all the yarn at once. There are no dye lots, and you can make it with as many skeins as you want, depending on size."

"I love that idea," I replied, envisioning a large, cozy blanket. "Can I get started now?" I handed Patricia a multi-colored skein.

"Absolutely. Do you want me to ball it?"

"Yes, please."

She took the skein and placed it on an umbrella swift. She then passed the yarn through a hand-cranked ball winder. The process took the large round hank of yarn and stretched it out wide like a giant spider-web. It reminded me of a huge wooden hand stretching its fingers. The yarn was draped over all the outstretched wooden pegs. As Patricia cranked it, a high-pitched wheedling rose up and the fingers spun in a circle. The hank of yarn was slowly wound into a seamless and symmetrical ball, perfect for hand knitting. Patricia placed the ball in a clear bag with the shop logo on the front.

"Hey, Patricia," exclaimed a girl pushing a stroller up to the door.

"Hello, Heather." Patricia handed me the bag and walked to the door to help let her in. "And hello little Harlan!" Patricia bent down and put her hand into the stroller. I could hear a small giggle.

"Hi Jane," said Heather with a smile.

"Hi."

"What's different about you, Heather?" asked Patricia.

"Oh, please, can't you tell?" she asked.

"Your bangs!" said Patricia. "They're cute."

"I hate them," said Heather, wiping her hand across her forehead. "I keep trying to brush them aside so people don't notice." They fell back into place. She pursed her lips and tried puffing them away. They rose and gently fell back. "They keep getting in my face. They tickle my nose."

Heather was a slender, black-haired young mother. She was very pretty and her bangs accentuated her cute face and turned-up nose.

"I like them as well," I said.

"So do I," said Chris, coming in from sitting outside.

"Thanks, Chris, but you are all being sweet. I think I look crazy," Heather said. "You know, like Angelina Jolie in *Girl Interrupted* crazy; like, they're-going-to-institutionalize-me crazy."

"You look great!" said Patricia, laughing. "Doesn't your mommy look great, Harlan?" She cooed at the little infant in the stroller.

"I just feel like such a...mom," said Heather, taking a seat at the table.

"You *are* a mom," said Patricia.

"I know, but I don't want to look like one."

"Oh please," said Chris. "You're still hot."

"*That's* why I love coming to this shop," replied Heather.

"Me too," I said, "and I haven't even been complimented today."

"Well, you're hot too," said Chris with a chuckle.

"And what about me?" asked Patricia.

"You sell me yarn," said Chris. "You're smoking hot," he said, laughing.

PATRICIA AND ADAM SCRIBNER

We all took seats near Heather around the wooden table. The afternoon sun moved its way across the bay window. The window's refraction laid out a bright square of light along the floor, and moved in the opposite direction across our feet. Kids started getting out of school, and we could hear them yelling and running down the sidewalk outside. Once in a while I'd glance up from my knitting and look outside. I'd see a group of a young students staring at us through the window. They would dart aside when I looked up. The kids were carrying their lightweight jackets in their arms: a sure sign of warm weather.

Around four, Trish's husband, Adam, came in.

"Hi honey." He walked over to the counter where Trish was and kissed her. "And hey, Jane! Seeing you here a lot lately! What's going on?"

"Nothing much."

"Jane is starting on a blanket like this one," Trish said, holding up the one I had looked at. "The one we did for the Homeless Shelter Auction."

"Nice!" Adam said.

"I really love the pattern," I said.

"No work today, Jane?"

"I got out early."

"So, first thing on the to-do list is head over to the knit shop, eh?" he teased.

I laughed. "How could I stay away?"

"Where do you work?" he asked.

"I work at a physical therapy office in the Village."

"The Village. That's a nice place to work."

"It is. I love the Village, but I feel like I've been spending fewer and fewer days in the city."

"Really?"

"Yeah. Ever since I found this knitting shop and *you guys*, I feel like I haven't had anything to do over in New York except go to work. My home is here now, most of my friends are here now. There are good *bars* here."

"Ah, we've stolen you away from the big city," said Adam.

"No, I don't think you've stolen me. It's just my old life – well, after I graduated from NYU – revolved so much around Dennis and work, Dennis and work"

"Oh, you went to NYU."

"Yes. Yeah."

"When did you graduate? Not too long ago, I'm guessing."

"About three years ago."

"Oh, ok. You wouldn't happen to know Ken Forman, would you?

"No…I don't think so. NYU's pretty big."

"I know. Just thought I'd try. He was a former student of mine. I think he graduated fairly recently."

"You're a teacher."

"Adam teaches science," Trish said.

"That's cool," I said. "I used to tutor English when I was in college."

"That's why you are so good with words," said Patricia.

"Maybe," I replied, feeling like I should have said something witty.

"Well we're really happy to have you here in Hoboken, Jane. We love it when you come by the shop. Don't we, Trish? Everyone talks about how much they love the new girl."

"Really?"

"Oh, yes."

"You guys are sweet," I said sincerely. "I didn't find anything like this place in New York."

"Well, Hoboken is a lot smaller," Adam posited. "It's more like a neighborhood or town. People sharing the same interests are more concentrated in one place. I like to call it 'city-living lite.'"

"Well, I don't know what to call it, but I don't know what I would do without you guys- especially, when I first moved here." I turned in my seat to face Trish.

"Back in Manhattan, there wasn't a place anything like this. I had friends – a lot of them stayed in Manhattan after college. But I definitely didn't have any friends who knit – besides Rachel, who you have yet to meet. But here, everything revolves around knitting. It's a whole community based on knitting."

"That's exactly what we hoped it would be," said Trish.

"It's a third space," said Adam.

"A what?" said Trish.

"Well, everyone has their home and their work, but they need a third space – somewhere where they can go for a shared activity – whether it's a restaurant, or a softball field, or a shop like Trish's."

"Or a bar," said Trish.

"Well, look at a lot of TV shows," Adam continued. "A lot of them do take place in that 'third space.' *Cheers* – the bar, the only setting on the show. We have no idea where any of the characters live. The only vestiges of work are displayed in Norm's mailman costume. *Friends* – another example – would flip between the apartment – the home space – to that café – what was it called?"

"Central Perk," I said, remembering years of *Friends*-watching on VHS.

"Right! – Central Perk – that was their shared third space."

"You ever watch *Frasier*? A big favorite of my dad's," I said.

"Sure."

"Well, they would flip from Kelsey Grammar's Seattle apartment to his radio station, and then to the coffee shop, where he and Niles and Daphney would hash out all their issues over lattes."

"Exactly. The third space pops up all over the place," said Adam.

"That's really interesting. That's definitely what this place has become."

"For all of us."

"Honey," Trish said matter-of-factly. "I work here."

"Yeah, but you know." Adam smiled at his wife.

"It is my job," she said.

"Yes, but don't you think of it as a place away from home? For instance, you're not working during knit nights."

"I think of it as my place of work, but also a place where my friends can meet me. But, primarily, I am a shop owner here. Half of the people we know in Hoboken we wouldn't have met if they hadn't been customers first."

"True."

"Trish, what did you do before you opened the shop?"

"Something I liked a whole lot less than this, finance."

"Wow. Big change," I said.

"No kidding," replied Trish. "I haven't had a migraine in years!"

"I like that third-space idea," I said to Adam.

"Give Nora Ephron all the credit," he replied.

"Reading Nora Ephron lately?" Patricia teased.

"Might be, might be." Adam replied. "Got to catch up on my chick-lit. No, I heard her on NPR on my way to work."

"Right," said Trish. "We know you are always the one that wants to watch *You've Got Mail*."

"The yarn shop always brings out my tough side," replied Adam. "I'm going to go watch football now."

My cell phone rang. "Sorry, Adam and Trish – I have to take this. It's my dad." I stepped outside and put the phone to my ear. "Hey, Dad."

"Hi honey. I was wondering if we could have dinner tonight?"

"Sure. Where?"

"How about I come to you. You pick the place. Let's say sevenish. I'll meet you at your apartment."

"Sounds great. See you then."

"You know, we're practically neighbors now."

"I know! I love having you so close."

"I'll just, I'll just come on down to yer neck o' the woods," he said in his best southern accent.

"Ha, ok, Dad."

"Love you, honey."

"Love you too."

With my father coming to town, I wanted to get home quickly. I knew my apartment was a mess and I didn't want my father to see it that way. I also needed to put on something nicer to wear, knowing that my father, as usual, would show up wearing a sport coat.

I ducked back inside the shop and grabbed my things.

"Adam, Trish, Heather – so nice to see you all. And it was nice meeting you, Chris. Adam, we'll continue our third space conversation. Maybe we'll start a Nora Ephron book club. Another third space we can share!"

 "Anytime, Jane," Adam said laughing "Wonderful seeing you. Hope to see you soon."

***

My phone rang again while I was in the shower. Thinking it was my dad stuck in traffic, I jumped out quickly to answer it. It was Andrew.

"Hey Jane, what are you doing right now?" he asked.

Embarrassed to be answering the phone naked, I said, "Nothing." The shower was still running.

"I'd like to see you," he said.

"When?"

My call waiting beeped. *No, not now.*

"Tonight."

"I can't tonight, I've got a date."

"A date! With whom?"

"My dad," I told him, laughing. My phone beeped again. "Andrew I have to go, I will call tomorrow. I miss you."

"Ok. Call me," he said.

I clicked my call-waiting button. "You can't park in this city," said my dad.

"You *drove*?! Why did you drive? You're only a light rail station away!"

"I drove," he said, as if that were reason enough.

"Let me meet you at the parking garage on Fourth – next to the hospital. Gotta go, Dad. I'm just getting out of the shower."

"See you in a minute, honey," he said.

I had cleaned up my apartment just for my dad's visit. Now, I was meeting him at the garage.

"It's impossible to find parking here," he said to me getting out of his car. "I drove around for twenty minutes."

"That's what happens when you drive into town on a Friday night, Dad," I replied.

My dad looked sharp. His gray hair was perfectly combed to the side. His tall frame looked thin in a three-button green sport coat and dark blue polo shirt.

"That's one very green coat," I said.

"I feel like I won the Masters when I wear this," he replied.

"Well, you look very Spring. You look great."

"Thanks, honey." He put his arm around me and we walked to the restaurant.

"I feel like I barely see you and Mom anymore. And especially since you're not living with each other, it's like I see you half as much as I would normally."

"Yes, well. Where are we headed?" he asked, trying to veer the subject away from himself and Mom.

"O'Nieal's," I replied. "It's right up your alley."

We entered O'Nieal's Irish Pub. The place had the distinction of having my favorite burger in Hoboken. I also knew my father would want a Guinness. Guinness ads adorned the walls. "My Goodness My Guinness." "A Guinness a Day." "Guinness for Strength."

Waiting for our pints to arrive, I spoke to Dad about how happy I had become in my new city. I told him about the knit group, my easy commute to work, and about Marvin.

"I'm really proud of you, Jane," he said. "I used to worry about you when you were living with Dennis. I don't worry about you anymore."

I finally worked up the courage to ask him: "What happened with you and mom?"

"I don't know, Jane. I didn't want to leave, but she never acted like she cared about me – not the way she used to, anyway."

"What do you mean, Dad?"

"I still don't think she cares that I left."

I reached across the table and took his hand. I didn't know what to say. "Of course she cares! Every time I talk to her, she mentions the same thing!" Hearing myself say this, I wracked my brain for a time my mom had truly expressed the wish to have my dad back. I couldn't quite place an instance. But I was positive this was how she felt.

"Really, Jane? I doubt it."

"No! She does. When was the last time you talked?"

"Gosh." He sighed. "I don't know, Janie. I don't know. It seems like it's been a veritable age."

"Yes, I think it has. You need to pick up the phone and call her. Or go over and *see* her."

"As if she's tried to call me."

"Dad, *come on*. You and Mom are grown-ups. This is crazy: the two of you apart like this. If you want, I can come home and we can get the three of us together in one room. I feel like we haven't all been in one place since Christmas."

"Jane, I really don't think calling her would do a lot of good. I tried talking to her before I moved to the hotel."

"Really. What did you say?"

"You don't understand, Janie."

"What don't I understand? Why do you and Mom keep telling me that? Why am I so in the dark about all this?"

He grimaced. He looked like he was at a loss for words. He looked down at the table.

"I'm sorry," I said. "You're right. We don't have to talk about this."

"No, Jane, I know it's bothering you, too."

"Well, yes, of course it is. I love you both."

CURSE OF THE BOYFRIEND SWEATER

He sighed again.

"What aren't you telling me?" I asked.

"Nothing. Maybe you should try speaking to your mother. Maybe she has something she wants to tell you."

"What is that supposed to mean?"

"Nothing, Jane." He sighed. "Your mother…your mother is not what I thought she was, is all."

"Are you insulting Mom?"

"No! It's just… Jane, I don't think this is the time or the place for this discussion."

"Ok, Dad."

"You should talk to your mother yourself."

"Alright. I'll talk to mom."

"Did I tell you I shot an 88 at Hendrick's Field Golf Course," he said.

"That's great, Dad."

***

I was greeted at L and J's bar to a big "Hey!" Margaux, Jamison, Patricia, Adam, Chris, Mia, and

David were all standing at the back corner of the crowded space.

"It's about time you showed up," said Margaux.

"What can I get you?" Adam asked.

"How was dinner with dad?" asked Patricia.

"How's your blanket coming along?" asked Jamison.

"Red wine, and great!" I said over the noise of the crowd.

It felt good to be surrounded by friends. I started talking to Jamison about how thankful I was for the knit group.

"I feel the same way," she said. "I moved here three years ago and took a beginner's knitting class. I never expected to meet such a nice group of people. I just wanted to learn how to knit."

Margaux chimed in, "I know. I just wanted to learn a new hobby, you know, find a place other than bars to hang out in." She took a sip of beer and said, "that *kind of* worked."

"My friend Rachel would love you guys," I said.

"You should bring her by," said Margaux.

CURSE OF THE BOYFRIEND SWEATER

"I will," I said as Adam handed me a glass of red wine.

***

The next morning, I slept past 10. The sun was peeking through my curtains. I opened them, flooding my room with light. My window was open and the day was warm. I texted Rachel, "Hob arts n mus fest. Come over!"

She texted back, "too early. See you at 1!"

I was itching to get out of my apartment, so I left early.

I told Rachel I would meet her at the PATH train but it took me an extra ten minutes to navigate the crowds that had formed on Washington Street.

"I need energy," said Rachel, dragging me by the arm as we walked from the station into a coffee shop. Like me, Rachel had been out late the night before. She was on a date and didn't make it back to her loft until 1 am, though that's early by New Yorker standards. She was wearing oversized sunglasses, standard day-after-a-long-night-out apparel.

The Hoboken Arts and Music Festival had two lines of booths, each running seven blocks on either side of Washington Street. The booths were filled with artists and vendors peddling their wares. There were photographers, painters, sculptors, potters, and designers. And there was food, a lot of food. Booths were selling gyros, corn on the cob, sausage and pepper sandwiches, crab cakes, funnel cakes, cupcakes, and even deep fried Oreos.

We began sifting our way through the crowds of people. We could hear blues music coming from the stage set up in front of City Hall.

The temperature was hitting the high sixties for the first time so we picked up scoops of ice cream and walked through the crowd to Fourth Street.

"Want to meet The Knitters?" I asked, referring to my new friends.

"Finally," said Rachel. "I get to meet The Knitters."

We walked into the midst of a large crowd gathered inside Patricia's. There were a few regulars and a bunch of people I didn't recognize browsing the shop. I introduced Rachel to Chris, Heather, and Margaux, all of whom were sitting and knitting at the table.

"Very nice to meet you," said Heather.

"I've heard a lot about you," said Margaux.

CURSE OF THE BOYFRIEND SWEATER

"What did you tell them?" said Rachel, looking at me with a grin.

"Oh, nothing…" With that, I playfully turned my attention to Patricia and let them talk. "I need another skein for my blanket," I said, holding up a colorful tuft of yarn.

"Don't you love the pattern?" Patricia asked.

"I do, but I might need something other than wool to knit, since the weather is getting warmer," I said.

"Yes, it's that time of year."

Patricia balled the skein of yarn in her wooden machine and I sat down and began to knit another square for my blanket. The mitered squares took just enough concentration to make them challenging.

Rachel, meanwhile, was feeling her way around the shop. Every once in a while I would hear her say, "Oh, I *love* this," or, "this is *so soft*."

And, while we sat in the shop and knitted, the crowds outside were growing. More and more people kept passing Patricia's Yarns to get to the festival on Washington Street. A young couple, obviously tired from too much walking, sat down at the table and chairs outside of the shop.

"Oh god," said Trish, looking at them.

They opened a bag of sausage and pepper sandwiches and were drinking beers wrapped in brown paper bags.

"Classy," continued Patricia turning her attention back to her customers.

"That girl keeps licking her fingers," laughed Chris. "I bet they come in here next and start touching the yarn."

"They better not," replied Patricia. "Is it rude to give them handy-wipes?"

With their backs to the window, they were oblivious to that fact that we were watching their every move. At this point the boy was feeding bites of his sandwich to his girlfriend and kissing her. It sounded like, "I ruvv oo. Chomp."

"That's disgusting," Chris said under his breath. "Eww."

"They better not come in here and touch my yarn with their sausage fingers," said Patricia, standing at the back of the shop. "I don't want to have to change the name of this place from Patricia's Yarns to Bitch's Yarns."

The couple, hearing all the voices and laughter, turned and saw us looking at them through the large glass window. Embarrassed, they got up and left.

CURSE OF THE BOYFRIEND SWEATER

Rachel held up a skein of blue alpaca and said jokingly to Patricia, "Was I supposed to wash my sausage fingers before I touched this?"

"Not funny," Patricia replied.

We stayed at the shop and knitted until it closed. Rachel cast on yet another scarf.

"Seriously, another scarf?" I asked her.

"I just love starting new ones."

"You need to finish one soon. I've barely seen one of your scarves make it past the pot-holder phase."

"Well someone doesn't have the long commute from Jersey every day to keep up her knitting."

"Oh, please. As if I could ever finish anything during my PATH ride."

I fastened the remaining stitches of a block on my mitered square blanket.

As the shop was closing, Rachel and I said our goodbyes and strolled out.

"You were right, they are a great group." she said.

"And you only met a few of them," I replied and gave her a hug goodbye.

That night, I went home and took one last look at the cowl I had finished. It was lying near my bed. It was beautiful: silky and soft, and that wonderful deep gray. I put it in a box with a short note that said "Happy Mother's Day, Mom! I love you! *Jane.*"

BLANKET
Mitered Koigu Blanket

Charity Blanket

This mitered blanket is a variation of an age old theme designed for Koigu with instructions for blankets, small or large. You can knit as many squares as you like and come up with your own combination, or follow our guidelines to make our specific sizes. Whatever you choose, a Koigu blanket should be treasured.

Yarn: Koigu KPPPM, two colors (A-solid & B-multi)
2 hanks makes 4 blocks.
"Supersquares" consist of 4 blocks, 2 of one set, and 2 of another set.
A baby blanket takes 4 Supersquares. A large blanket takes 15.

CURSE OF THE BOYFRIEND SWEATER

Gauge 7 stitches = 1 inch using US3s
Square should measure 8x8 inches

For abbreviations, please see list at the end of the book.

Using A CO 112
Row 1: K53, ssk, [k2tog] twice, k to end.
Row 2: and all even rows: Purl
Row 3: K52, [ssk] twice, k2tog, k to end.
Row 5: K50, ssk, [k2tog] twice, k to end.
Row 7: K49, [ssk] twice, k2tog, k to end.
Row 9: Using Color B K47, ssk, [k2tog] twice, k to end. (97 remain)
Row 11: K46, [ssk] twice, k2tog, k to end.
Row 13: K44, ssk, [k2tog] twice, k to end.
Row 15: K43, [ssk] twice, k2tog, k to end.
Row 17: K41, ssk, [k2tog] twice, k to end.
Row 19: Using Color A K40, [ssk] twice, k2tog, k to end. (82 remain)
Row 21: K38, ssk, [k2tog] twice, k to end.
Row 23: K37, [ssk] twice, k2tog, k to end.
Row 25: K35, ssk, [k2tog] twice, k to end.
Row 27: K34, [ssk] twice, k2tog, k to end.
Row 29: Using Color B K32, ssk, [k2tog] twice, k to end. (67 remain)
Row 31: K31, [ssk] twice, k2tog, k to end.
Row 33: K29, ssk, [k2tog] twice, k to end.
Row 35: K28, [ssk] twice, k2tog, k to end.
Row 37: K26, ssk, [k2tog] twice, k to end.
Row 39: Using Color A K25, [ssk] twice, k2tog, k to end. (52 remain)
Row 41: K23, ssk, [k2tog] twice, k to end.

Row 43: K22, [ssk] twice, k2tog, k to end.

Row 45: K20, ssk, [k2tog] twice, k to end.

Row 47: K19, [ssk] twice, k2tog, k to end.

Row 49: Using Color B K17, ssk, [k2tog] twice, k to end. (37 remain)

Row 51: K16, [ssk] twice, k2tog, k to end.

Row 53: K14, ssk, [k2tog] twice, k to end.

Row 55: K13, [ssk] twice, k2tog, k to end.

Row 57: K11, ssk, [k2tog] twice, k to end.

Row 59: Using Color A K10, [ssk] twice, k2tog, k to end. (22 remain)

Row 61: K8, ssk, [k2tog] twice, k to end.

Row 63: K7, [ssk] twice, k2tog, k to end.

Row 65: K5, ssk, [k2tog] twice, k to end.

Row 67: K4, [ssk] twice, k2tog, k to end.

Row 69: Using Color B K2, ssk, [k2tog] twice, k to end. (7 remain)

Row 71: ssk, Sl 1, k2tog, psso, k2tog

Row 73: Sl 1, k2tog, psso

Fasten off remaining stitch.

Chapter 14: Knitting on the Pier

As the cool weather of Spring gave way to the warmer weather of Summer, the pansies and daffodils began to wither.

I loved Hoboken in Summer. With my windows open, I could smell the roasting garlic from the Italian restaurant down the street (or was it coming from Mrs. Genovese, below?), and the salty air coming off the Hudson River. During the winter and spring, the Hudson was too cold and too windy to walk along, but during the summer, the waterfront walkway was crowded with people strolling and enjoying the view of New York City. I could see everything from the Empire State building, the Chrysler building, and the lights of Times Square, which seemed to send a huge fuzzy glow over midtown at night, especially on hot, hazy evenings.

My father would say, "I can't believe this is the same Hoboken I would come to when we were kids. We used to throw rocks at the windows of abandoned factories."

Hoboken had definitely changed.

Hoboken was a waterfront town: its economy was firmly rooted in transportation. The soldiers of World War I declared, "Heaven, Hell, Or Hoboken," upon shipping out from its docks. The rail yard and train station used to be the end of the line for passengers riding eastbound from the lower 48 states (after that, people would ferry to New York City). By the mid-20th Century, however, Hoboken's waterfront was unable to accommodate the larger ships of the time. When freighters began to prefer the deeper, wide-open harbor space of Brooklyn's docks, Hoboken fell into a depression and its infrastructure fell into disrepair.

But all that changed in the 1980s. Young people – mostly artists and musicians – started to flee the high rents of New York City and gave rise to a wave of gentrification. Old factories were refurbished into high-end luxury condos, and ferries once again carried people back and forth across the Hudson. As more people moved in, more open space was needed, and so large parks were built onto piers that stretched out into the Hudson River.

One such park was Pier A. It stretched far out towards Manhattan. The river pounded against the ballast securing the pier to the bedrock below. The pier seemingly had acres of grass and trees and marble walkways and stairs.

The trees in the park grew in a kind of slate-gray hash, like the stuff they use on clay tennis courts. I was always amazed that trees could grow in it. The vertical cylinders of the trees jutting out from the planar shelf of gray gave a modern feel to the park, as if it were a geometric forest, a forest grown in the middle of a city – which is essentially what it is. Cement giving birth to foliage.

There was a glass flame monument to the Hoboken victims of September 11th. People placed roses on the pedestals left in the space between the edges.

People sunned on the grass, played games, watched ships sail by from the far end of the pier, and cast out lines from the pier's edge to fish for stripers.

Most importantly, it was a perfect setting for summertime knitting.

I had put knitting the wool blanket on hold for a little while and had started a new project: something for a baby. P.A. Jess was expecting again so "The Knitters" decided to make a few things for her. I settled on a baby sweater. Because I didn't know the gender yet (Jess decided to do things the old fashioned way and not find out if it would be a boy or girl), I chose a beautiful Rowan turquoise organic cotton and wool blend yarn to knit.

I met the girls on the pier on a sunny afternoon. "It's a beautiful day," I said and sat down on a large cotton blanket that Margaux had brought from home.

Pier A was filled with people. We sat under a tree in the shade. Every now and then, cute, shirtless boys

would throw their Frisbee near us and have to
retrieve it. *Were they doing that on purpose*?

"If P.A. Jess walks by, I hope everyone has
something else in their bags to knit. I'm pretty sure
she'd find it strange if she saw us all knitting baby
clothes," said Margaux. "Unless any of you have
something to share? Ladies?"

My backup was the mitered blanket – I always
carried skeins of Koigu in my purse.

When I found out P.A. Jess was expecting, I couldn't
help but begin an adorable sweater for the new baby.
The sweater I chose was a cute cardigan, which I
could knit in one piece from the top down. It's so
much fun to make and comes together without a
seam.

The yarn was gorgeous, and the perfect weight;
neither too heavy, nor too light. I cast on using size 6
circulars. But, unlike the cowl, this yarn was knitting
up quickly on sixes.

"You going out with Andrew tonight?" asked
Margaux.

"Yes," I said with a smile, my needles clicking away.

"Very nice." she said. "Where you going?"

"Union Square Café."

"Oh, how very romantic," said Margaux.

A cruise ship slowly sailed down the river, past the pier. You could see the passengers waving. There was a small group of people standing on the end of the pier waving back.

"I wonder where they're heading?" I asked.

"I don't know, but I'd rather be here," Chris said.

***

Union Square Café sat right on a corner near Union Square Park. There was a farmer's market there every day in the summer. That night, I had hoped to get to Union Square before Andrew so that I could peruse the market, but my feet, in a great but slightly uncomfortable pair of heels, had other plans. I waited at the bar in the restaurant for Andrew to arrive.

Andrew walked in looking like one of the Kennedy brothers after a day of summering in Hyannis Port. A blue pinstriped shirt and a navy sport coat looked great against his tanned complexion.

"You look gorgeous," he said to me and kissed my cheek. I was also wearing navy, a cute sleeveless dress and white heels.

"So do you," I said.

"Can I get you another drink?"

"Yes, please," I said and slid my empty glass towards the bartender. "Dirty martini, please."

"I love a girl that drinks a martini," said Andrew.

"A *dirty* martini," I said with a deviant smile and a laugh.

"I'll have a Macallan rocks," said Andrew to the bartender. He stood next to my barstool and placed his hand on the small of my back.

"Have you been here before?" he asked.

"No. It's beautiful," I said. The restaurant had high ceilings, large framed prints of the ocean and mirrors on the walls. Its tall columns reminded me of an old bank. The aromas from the kitchen made my mouth water from the second I stepped in the front door.

We were seated at a table for two outside. My seat faced the park. People walked at a brisk New York pace past our table as we sat and ate. It's one of the things I love about New York: having a calm dinner surrounded by people in such a hurry. Everyone around us racing in a thousand directions, down to the subway, past the garbage-can-drummers perched on the park steps, through the market; the different paces that everyone keeps, the bustle of a million lives superimposed on each other existing in one tiny island.

From the moment we sat down, we were never at a loss for words. He told me about his job, that his work had been very hectic and demanding as of late. He told me that although he had a lot of friends, he, a Seattle boy, still felt lonely because he didn't have any family that lived close to New York City.

"I've been living away from home since Fordham. I only saw my parents three times a year during college, and even less after I graduated. My grandparents live just west of Mount Rainier, my brother in Southern California, my sister in Texas. I want to be able to see them, or at least have time to see them if they come visit in New York. More than anything, though, I want to see you more."

"I want to see more of you, too," I said grasping his hand from across the table.

"I work too much," he said. "I need to take more time off. Business is so demanding lately."

"You should learn to knit," I joked. "It's good for stress."

"Maybe," he said laughing.

I told him about the situation with my parents. "At our age," I said, "I figured I would be able to understand why relationships don't always work out."

"The older I get, the more I realize that my parents are just as flawed as I am," he said.

We talked about relationships, his advertising firm, my office, and Andrew's interest in art and design – one of the reasons he went into advertising in the first place. It was obvious Andrew was a very sensitive and caring person. He cared very much about his family and friends. I liked that about him.

"Come to my place for a drink?" He asked.

My heart began to beat faster. "Yes."

***

The next morning I received a text from Rachel: "call me."

"Hey lady," I said when she picked up the phone.

"You sound happy."

"I am. What's going on?" I asked.

"Nothing. We just haven't talked in a while. You've been ditching me for all those knitting bitches in Hoboken," she joked.

"I know, I know. We'll get together soon."

An ambulance drove by. The siren blared into my ears and phone.

"Where are you?" Rachel asked.

"I'm walking home," I said.

"Home from *where*?"

"…Um…Andrew's," I said quietly.

"Oh my god. Did someone spend the night?" she asked, laughing.

"Maybe," I replied.

"Good for you, Jane," she replied. "You deserve to be happy. What happened last night?"

I told Rachel how gorgeous Andrew was and how he was such a gentleman. I told her about dinner, and how he invited me to his apartment in SOHO.

"Be careful Jane," she said. "I don't want you to get your heart broken again."

"I know. I'll be careful. I am not knitting him anything."

"Good girl," she said.

"What's going on with you?" I asked.

"You're not the only one who meets cute men. I met one too," she replied.

"Rachel! Tell me about him."

"I'd love to, but I have to go. I'm getting on the subway now. You're not the only one on her way home this morning."

P.A. JESS'S BABY SWEATER

P.A.'s Baby Sweater

This cardigan is a great size that can fit for a good period of time. The sizing is generous and the 3 buttons make it easy to put on & take off. The cotton/wool blend of yarn makes it great to wear for most seasons.

CURSE OF THE BOYFRIEND SWEATER

Baby Cardigan, 12-18 Month Size
Yarn: Amy Butler for Rowan
Needles: US 3 & 5
Gauge: 22 sts = 4 inches in St. st.
Notions: markers, tapestry needle, stitch holders, 3 buttons.
For abbreviations, please see list at end of book.

PATTERN
Using a #3 needle, CO 75
Work in Seed st. slipping 1st st. every row for 3 rows.
Buttonhole: next row, work 2 sts., YO, K2 Tog, work in seed st. to last 4 sts. P2 tog, YO, P1, K1.
Seed 4 more rows.
(Make 2 more buttonholes, 2" apart as you work the sweater.)

Change to #6 needle.
Setup raglan – be mindful to keep first and last 4 sts of row in seed stitch for button band while body of sweater is worked in st. st.
Seed 4, pm, K12, m1, pm, k1, pm, m1
K7, m1, pm, k1, pm, m1
K25, m1, pm, k1, pm, m1
K7, m1, pm, k1, pm, m1
K12, pm, seed 4
1. Seed 4, Purl, seed 4
2. *Work to seam st., m1, yo, m1, repeat from * 3 times more, work to end.

Repeat last 2 rows 13 times more, ending with a right side row. 195 sts remain.

Divide:

F-31 (1) S-37 (1) B-55 (1) S-37 (1) F-31

Purl across front to first marker (not including button band marker).

Slip sts from first marker to sleeve, inc seam.
St. on other side of holder (39 sts.)
Cast on 4 sts.
Purl across back 55 sts.
Slip next seam to seam sleeve sts onto holder.
CO 4 sts.
Purl to end 125 sts.
Work body St st. until measures 6 ½"
Change 8 rows seed. – BO in pattern loosely.

SLEEVES
Place 39 held sts onto needle.
With yarn, pick up and knit two sts, pm, pick up and knit 2 more (43 sts)
Knit for 2 ½"
Next rnd – decrease before and after marker as follows:
knit to marker, slip marker, k1, k2 tog, knit to 3 sts before marker, SSK, k1
Continue decreasing every 8th round (approx. every 1")
Total of 5 decreases – 33 sts remain.

CURSE OF THE BOYFRIEND SWEATER

Change to seed stitch for 8 rows.
BO loosely
use a needle 1mm larger to bind off

Chapter 15: Leaves Fall in Hoboken

By fall, Andrew and I were spending more and more
time together.

I was getting nervous that maybe we were becoming
too serious. I made it a point to keep going out with
Rachel and The Knitters to keep my personal life my
own. With Dennis, my life became his life. I never
wanted that to happen again.

In the summer, there was always room at the table to
knit at Patricia's Yarns. But in the fall, all that
changed. It seemed as if everyone could feel the
weather changing, the cool winds picking up, and
the desire to knit greatly increased. As bears stock up
on food to hibernate, knitters grab their needles and
cast on new hats, mittens, sweaters, and wool socks
to get ready for winter.

I rarely saw Patricia sitting down. She was almost
always helping customers find a pattern, ball yarn,
or figure out how many skeins it would take to make
a sweater.

On one such day, I was walking into the yarn shop
as The Knitters were leaving.

"How about we grab the big outdoor table at
O'Nieal's?" I heard Margaux say. "Hey Jane, you
want to come?"

"Thanks," I said. I was planning on knitting at the shop, but, peeking through the window and seeing the overflow of customers, I turned back to Margaux. "You bet."

We followed Margaux down Fourth Street to O'Nieal's. It was a beautiful and sunny fall evening: a perfect evening to sit outside. Daylight Saving Time hadn't begun yet, so it was one of those fall evenings when the sun sets brilliantly for an hour. The clouds above Our Lady of Grace Church at the western edge of Church Square Park were ablaze with that golden glow of fall. To the right, the sky assumed a cold, gray-blue color, and I could imagine the buildings of New York just beginning to light up beneath it. The leaves were turning yellow and gold above us, and some were dropping lazily down onto our knitting. We grabbed an extra plastic chair for our table when Chris showed up and squeezed in between Jamison and Michelle. We ordered a round of Guinness.

"I don't feel guilty at all for drinking today," said Margaux, holding up her pint glass. "My fiancé and I had to meet with our priest in West Orange this morning about getting married in a Catholic church. It didn't go well because he's not Catholic."

"The priest isn't Catholic?" asked Jamison, grinning mischievously.

"No! My fiancé isn't Catholic, smartass," laughed Margaux.

"Who was the priest?" asked Chris.

"Father Anthony," said Margaux. "Why?"

"Oh no," said Chris.

"What?" insisted Margaux.

"Nothing," said Chris.

"Come on!"

"It's just, I grew up in West Orange," said Chris. "Father Anthony was my priest."

"So?" inquired Margaux.

"Well, I used to work at this bar in the city and served him drinks," he said.

"What's wrong with that?" I asked.

"I worked at the Boot," he said.

"Holy crap!" said Margaux, almost spitting out her beer.

"What's 'The Boot'?" asked Michelle, still not understanding.

Chris raised his eyebrows, still laughing. "The Boot is a, shall we say, *all-male establishment*."

"Ohhh," said Michelle.

"Yeah," Chris continued. "We served drinks in our undies. Not exactly the type of place I was expecting to see my priest."

The waitress came over, reached an arm between Jamison and me and stacked our empty pint glasses together. "Another round?" she asked.

"Absolutely," said Patricia, walking up to our outdoor table. She had just closed the shop for the night. "Riley is with Adam, what's going on?"

"Good stories," I said. "Take a seat."

The sun was setting and the twinkling O'Nieal's lights, wrapped snakelike around all the trees surrounding the patio, began to luminesce, we decided to carry on to another place and paid our tab.

Only blocks away, Galligan's was a quintessential Irish pub. Framed pictures of castles and soccer players hung on the wall. Hurling sticks hung above the bar. Scarves embroidered with the names of soccer teams hung from the ceiling. The numerous TVs were all showing soccer and rugby games.

Although it was a weekend night, the clientele was mostly male ex-pats.

When we arrived, a cute bartender with an English accent asked, "Can I get you ladies a drink?"

"A round of Guinness," said Michelle.

"That round's on me," said a good-looking Irishman sitting at the end of the bar.

"That's not necessary," said Michelle bashfully.

The gentleman looked directly at the bartender and said, "That one's on me."

The bartender looked at Michelle and said, "Sorry, this round's on John, he's the owner." He thumbed in the Irishman's direction.

"Cheers!" we all said, looking the Irishman's way, amazed at our good fortune.

The Irishman eventually made his way down to our group. He was a handsome older man, probably in his mid-forties. He was well dressed in a white button-down shirt and designer jeans. He reminded me of an Irish Bruce Willis.

"Always nice to see a group of girls drinking Guinness," he said directly to me in his Irish brogue.

CURSE OF THE BOYFRIEND SWEATER

"My dad taught me to like the good stuff," I said holding up my pint to him. "Thank you."

"Haven't seen ya in me bar before," he said.

"No, this is my first time here." I could see all of my friends looking at us.

"I'm John," he said and held out his hand to me.

"Jane," I replied, and took his hand. "Nice to meet you."

"Lemme kno' if ya need anyting," he said to me, with a nod to my friends, and walked back to the end of the bar.

I walked back closer to my friends.

"He's cute," they all agreed. I blushed.

John smiled. He seemed pleased that there was a large group of girls in his pub. And we certainly weren't complaining about free drinks.

It was hard to tell what time it was in the dark pub. As it got later, the bar got louder and more crowded. I had more to drink, but I was having fun.

I was handed what would be my last pint when the door opened and two men in suits walked in.

"Those two look cute," said Jamison to me.

"Oh my god," I said to myself looking directly at them. I couldn't believe it. It was Andrew…and Dennis. "Oh my god," I said again. *What were they doing here? What were they doing together?* I turned my back to them, afraid that they would notice me.

I heard their voices as they walked past me. I hid in the middle of the huddle of my friends. I turned and saw them both shake hands with John, who stood up from his bar stool to greet them. Others were talking to me, but I wasn't listening. I couldn't for the life of me figure out what they were doing together.

I didn't hear what anyone else was saying. I finished my drink in a gulp. I wanted to stay calm. I wanted to be mature. I wanted to keep my emotions separate.

"What are you doing here?" I finally said loudly walking toward them, the beer getting the best of me.

"Jane, Hi," said Andrew, obviously startled.

"Wait, Andrew. Tell me this isn't the Jane you've been talking about?" laughed Dennis loudly.

"What are you doing with him? With Dennis," I asserted to Andrew, pointing my finger at Dennis. I knew I had had too much to drink. I could feel tears welling up in my eyes.

Dennis interrupted. "Why are you wasting your time with her?"

"Jane, I…" said Andrew.

"Jane, why don't you go back to your friends," said Dennis.

"I can't believe you're friends with him!"

"I didn't know this is the same Dennis," said Andrew.

"What difference does it make," said Dennis laughing. "It figures she would wind up in Jersey."

"Why are you such a jerk?" I said to Dennis, my voice beginning to crack.

"Let's talk about this," said Andrew.

"No, she's crazy," said Dennis, putting a hand on his shoulder. "Let's get a drink."

"Andrew," I said.

"We can talk outside," said Andrew looking directly at me.

"What is there to talk about, Jane?" responded Dennis. "Why don't you go cry someplace else."

"Why don't you go screw yourself, Dennis!" I screamed.

I turned and pushed past my friends who were now crowded near me and made my way through the busy bar. I pushed open the door and could feel my tears freeze in the cold night air. I couldn't believe what had just happened. I covered my mouth with my hand as I stood in the cold, and waited.

Andrew will come and talk to me, right? Andrew will come outside.

Seconds felt like minutes.

Finally, a hand touched my shoulder. "Let me walk you home," said Patricia.

***

The next morning there were no text messages on my phone. There was only one voicemail, from my mother. She wanted to get together for dinner later in the week. There was nothing from Andrew.

I sat on the edge of my bed holding my throbbing head. *How could Andrew be friends with Dennis?* I flopped my head back on my pillow.

CURSE OF THE BOYFRIEND SWEATER

Like watching an old VHS tape, I kept trying to
replay what had happened the night before. The
images were grainy and unclear.

I didn't want to talk to anyone. I didn't know what
to say to Andrew. I just wanted to be under my
covers. The windows were open and cool air flowed
into the apartment. I pulled the blankets over my
head. I kept waiting for my phone to beep, but it
never did.

Chapter 16: Back to Work

A rainy Monday morning didn't bother me at all. In fact, I looked forward to getting back to work, back to a routine. I always liked how the details of my job helped me to forget problems. It was a new day, even if it was cold and rainy. And besides, Mondays were Marvin days. I looked forward to seeing my new favorite patient.

But, as I helped Marvin onto the table in Room One, he burst out with some bad news of his own: "They're moving me out this weekend, Jane."

Within seconds, my problems seemed insignificant.

"Marvin, I am so sorry to hear that. What are you going to do?"

"I'm not sure. An agency has found me a shared room until I figure things out, but it won't be my home. I've been living in the same place for 22 years. Why is everyone so greedy?"

"I don't know. Sometimes it seems that way, though," I said.

"They're moving me to Yonkers," he said.

I paused and looked at Marvin. "Yonkers? Will you still be coming to our 14th Street office?"

"I don't suppose you make house calls?" he asked.

"I don't know what to say. You're my favorite. You're my knitter!"

"I know. I don't want to go. I've lived in Manhattan for so long. I've never even been to Yonkers. They said it was the only thing I could afford and still be able to get treatments."

"I'll miss you," I said.

"I want to show you something." He pulled up his pant leg. He was wearing the socks I gave him. "Thanks for these."

"Oh, Marvin." I could feel tears welling up inside me. I felt terrible - an arthritic old man being forced to give up his home. I gave him a big hug. "It'll be ok."

"I don't know, Jane."

I didn't know what else to say.

By the time he was leaving, rain was beating down on the windows facing 14th Street.

"Where's your umbrella?" I asked as we were walking to the elevator.

"I don't have one," Marvin answered. "Don't worry. There are always umbrellas right here." In true Marvin style, he snatched an umbrella from the umbrella stand next to the office door.

"Marvin, those are other people's umbrellas."

"Ahh, there are plenty left."

"Good bye, Marvin," I said as he walked slowly onto the elevator. "I'm going to miss you."

He smiled to me as he held up his new umbrella. "Just keep knitting, Jane! I'll knit something for you, too." The doors closed and down he went.

By the end of the day, the rain hadn't eased at all. It was lashing the pavement in huge swaths, bouncing off the cold fall cement, beating soggy sidewalk detritus into literal pulp. *I'm glad Marvin took an umbrella.*

"Jane, have a nice evening – I'll see you tomorrow," said Mark, rushing to the door.

"In a hurry?"

"No, just want to get home fast and stay dry."

"O.K. See you tomorrow."

"Dammit!" Mark said, rummaging through the umbrella stand. "Someone took my umbrella."

I grabbed mine from the stand. "You're fast, right?" I laughed.

Mark took a deep breath, stepped on the elevator, and put his hood up on his coat. "I hate Mondays," he said.

The storm didn't let up on my walk home, either. Despite my umbrella, my sneakers were soaked by the time I made it back to my apartment. I plucked off my soggy socks and threw them in the hamper. I put on a fresh pair from my drawer, a pair not too different from those I had made Marvin. They were soft and long and stretched halfway up my shins. I wiggled my toes in the warm wool.

With the rain keeping time on my windowsill, it wasn't hard for me to pass hours sitting on my couch knitting. Over the course of the evening, I made another square for my blanket.

After I had pulled the last stitch of the square taught, and tied off the last end, I felt it was time to talk about what had happened with Andrew and Dennis. I called Rachel.

"Why do I keep attracting guys like this?" I asked her.

"I can't believe that in a city of 8 million people, you date two that are friends."

"I didn't just date them," I said. "I lived with Dennis for three years."

"Are you going to call Andrew?" she asked.

"I don't know," I said. "I like to think I am stronger than I am. I can't believe I cried in front of them. I'm not calling him. I'm too good to date men like that." I asserted.

"You are!" said Rachel.

"I still can't believe they are friends."

"Why not, Jane? They work in the same field. They are both the same age. They live in the same city. Let's face it, you like a certain type," she said.

"No I don't. Not him. Not guys like him!" I said.

"Maybe Andrew is different," said Rachel.

"Maybe he's not," I replied. "What were they doing in *Hoboken?* Dennis never used to leave the city except on business. For him to come all the way to Andrew's old home they *must* be friends. You have no idea of the derogatory way he spoke about New Jersey to me. He used to say I came from the state that made Chernobyl look like pristine forest. He *never* would have let Andrew bring him to New Jersey unless they were really good friends. The first time he came home with me to meet my parents at our house he held his nose for half the train ride, which he thought was hilarious. He's such a jerk."

I hadn't thought about Dennis in months, but talking to Rachel about him made a whole well of unpleasant feelings rise up in me. Seeing him with Andrew was some sort of twisted proof of the type of guy that I date. And Andrew was supposed to be a kind of protection against that. He had been so sweet, such a gentleman; but seeing him with Dennis made me question everything.

"What should I do?" I asked.

"You need more time, Jane," she said.

"That advice sounds familiar."

"Seriously, you met Andrew pretty quickly after Dennis cheated. You need to take time and think about things."

"What about Andrew?" I asked.

"He'll understand if he really cares," she said.

"Maybe he'll call. But if he doesn't then he was more like Dennis than you thought."

Chapter 17: Bruce

"So who's going to help me out with the Hoboken Homeless Shelter auction?" asked Patricia at knit night.

"I will," said Mia.

"Me too!" joined Margaux.

"What are we knitting this year?" asked Chris.

"This year we are going to do things a little bit differently," Patricia said. "I would like for the group to submit multiple projects. I know that last year we did a group blanket, but the shelter needs more help this year. The more items they have, the better."

"Are we still going to make a blanket?" asked Margaux.

"Are *you* volunteering to stitch it up after the squares are made?" replied Patricia.

Margaux let out a deep sigh. "Yeah, I'll do it," she said.

"Way to go, Margaux," I joked.

"Well, we're gonna need more than just a blanket," said Patricia. "So, I will donate the yarn for anything you knit for the auction. Scarves, mittens, hats, baby sets – anything you would like to knit, I'll pick up the cost of the yarn. Just give me some notice as to what you're thinking of making."

***

I was walking home from work and ran into Margaux and Mia. They were stapling a flyer to a telephone pole.

"What are you guys doing?" I asked.

"Patricia asked if we would help hang up the flyers for the auction," said Mia. She held the paper steady to the pole while Margaux stapled it. "The flyer!" she exclaimed. "Staple the *flyer*! Not my *finger*!"

"It's not my fault your big fingers keep getting in the way!" said Margaux, pushing hard on the staple gun. "How do you knit with those sausages?" She joked.

The flyer stated:

Hoboken Homeless Shelter Auction
Friday October 19th, 7-10pm
Teak Restaurant
Silent auction with many incredible items donated by local businesses
Open bar and passed hors d'oeuvres, $50 per person suggested donation
All proceeds benefit the Hoboken Homeless Shelter

"Need some help hanging these up?" I asked.

"No, but we'd love the company if you want to walk with us," said Mia.

"You got it," I said.

"Maybe you could trade places with Margaux and staple so she doesn't staple my fingers off."

"Or," said Margaux, "maybe you could hold the flyer so that I don't have such huge fingers getting in the way of my staples!"

It was a beautiful fall day. We spent the afternoon walking from telephone pole to telephone pole, hanging flyers on community boards and placing them on car windshields.

"I'm so excited for the auction," said Mia. "I'm making a matching baby blanket and booties."

"I've got a design I'm working on for a scarf, and I'm going to make a hat to go with it," said Margaux.

"What are you going to make?" asked Mia.

"I'm not sure yet," I fibbed. I wanted to keep my blanket a secret.

My cell phone rang. It was my mother.

"Hey honey," she said.

"Hi Mom, what's going on?" I asked, still walking next to my friends, my feet kicking fallen leaves.

"I was wondering if you are free for dinner tonight."

"Uh, yes, sure," I said. "But don't you have Mahjong?"

"Canceled. The woman who was supposed to host tonight had to go to a Bar Mitzvah or something."

"Ok. What time?"

"How about seven?" she asked.

"Sounds good," I said, deliberately being short so I didn't ignore my friends.

"I look forward to seeing you."

We finished putting up some more flyers, and then Mia said she had to head home. Margaux and I were going the same way, so we bid Mia adieu and walked together.

"So, Jane, did you hear yet about what happened after you left the bar the other night?"

Oh no. I was hoping the other knitters hadn't noticed my outburst too much. I was embarrassed. "You mean after I went running out?"

"You should have been there for what we did to that guy after you left."

"Oh god. What did you do?"

"Well, admittedly, I think I probably had as much as you had to drink, probably more actually. Anyway, after you went running out and Trish followed you outside, Michelle and I went up to that guy and were like, 'You giving our girl a problem?'"

"You didn't." I was laughing, but my hands were covering my mouth.

"Oh yes! We were getting all *Jersey* - in his face, like, 'You got a problem with Jane, then you got a problem with *all of us.*'"

"Oh my God. No wonder Andrew hasn't called me."

"Wait, who's Andrew? I thought that was Dennis."

"*Andrew.* You know, like, Mr. Wonderful Boyfriend Who I Just Met Last Winter and Practically Was Falling For?"

"Ohhh, *Andrew.* Duh. Wait, he was there?"

"Yes! That's what was so upsetting. The two of them walked in *together*."

"Oh. Huh. I didn't realize that."

"Wait, which one did you tell off?" I panicked.

"Um, I don't know. He was shorter, maybe 5'10", short brown hair. I was kind of drunk, remember," she said.

"Whew. That was Dennis."

"But wait, that's not the end of it. He was like, 'Listen, ladies, you don't know Jane the way I do.' And I said, 'Jane is our friend, you're an ass.' Remember, I had a few drinks, wink wink. And he was like, 'Whoa! Simmer down now." Holding his hand in my face. 'The rodeo's out yonder.' And I said, 'What?' and I threw whatever I had left in my glass in his face. It went all over his suit jacket. Then, as he came out of his delirious *I can't believe you just ruined my jacket* stupor, he lunged at me."

"He did?"

"Yeah, grabbed my shirt, too. But I'm too quick, baby, and I jumped out of the way."

"Oh my god," I said. "I cannot believe this."

"Then Michelle said to him, 'Aw, your suit's stained. It looks like it needs a good washing.' And then *she* threw the rest of *her* drink in his face. 'The crowd loved it."

"No!"

"But then!" Margaux said. "But then, that cute Irishman, the bar owner, came over and said to Dennis, 'Oy, ye got a problem here?' Like really cool. Looking Dennis over and Dennis was, like, 'Yeah, I got a problem here'. The Irishman said, all cool-like 'Oy, didn't know it were rainin' outside.' And of course the crowd was eating it up."

"But then Dennis got furious and he actually tried to throw a punch at John. But John doesn't just look like Bruce Willis. He fights like him too. He blocked it and socked Dennis right in the gut. 'Dat's enuff o' dat now.' Whumpf! 'I'll be asking ye ter leave me bar, now, if ye don't mind.'" Margaux did a hilarious Irish accent. "Dennis didn't need any prodding. He slammed his beer on the bar so hard a crack shot down the middle of the glass, and he stormed out of the place."

"Holy. Crap." I said giggling.

"John apologized to us, but we apologized to him too. We just ended up leaving."

"At least John knows where his priorities are," I said.

"Better to take sides with pretty girls rather than one soggy guy!"

"God, Dennis is such…"

"Jerk," replied Margaux. "I can't believe you dated him for so long."

"Sometimes I can't believe it either. But, you know, he didn't usually act that way. I wonder what had him so upset."

"Well, either he just *really* loved that suit, or he might have been upset at seeing you with your new boyfriend."

"I doubt it."

As night fell, it began getting colder and colder. A strong wind was blowing through the streets.

When we got to Fifth Street, I said good- bye to Margaux and turned to go to my apartment.

At home, I changed into some warmer clothes and went out to meet my mom for dinner. We met at the parking garage, the usual rendezvous point of late. "Parking in this town is horrific," she said, stepping out of her car and slamming the door shut.

"I know, Mom," I said.

"And how are you?" she asked, locking her car.

"I'm ok," I said. "I like what you are wearing!" I reached my hand out to feel my mother's cowl, the one I sent her for Mother's Day.

"I told you I loved it when you gave it to me," she said.

"I know, but this is the first time I've seen you in it."

"Well, I've worn it many times. It looks great with everything."

"You look really good," I said. She seemed to have lost weight and looked more vibrant.

"Where would you like to go?"

"Let's go to Elysian Café," I said.

"Great," she replied. "Is Pat's Yarns still open?"

"It's Patricia's, Mom. Or, you can call her Trish. She hates being called Pat," I replied. "Something about the nuns at her Catholic school.   They used to call her Pat. And yes, it's open – if we hurry."

We walked into the shop just as David, Chris, and Heather were leaving.

"Hi, Jane," they said as they walked out together.

"We're headed to the park. You're welcome to join us."

"Thanks, but my mom and I haven't eaten yet," I said. "Do you want to get together later?"

"Absolutely," said Chris.

"Oh, Patricia, I love this," said my mother, wasting no time, lifting up a skein of baby alpaca yarn to her cheek. "This is so soft."

"That yarn just came in," said Patricia. "What are you looking to make?"

"I'm not sure," said my mother. "Maybe a hat?"

"What color were you thinking?" asked Patricia.

"I love this red," said Mom.

"You never wear red," I said curiously.

"Maybe it's not for me," she said, insinuating something.

"Is it for me?"

"Mmm...I don't know," said my mother, trying to hold back a smile.

"If it's not for me, then who is it for?" I asked.

"*Someone,*" she said with a grin.

Stomach turns. That *someone* was not me. And I'd wager a good hank of alpaca it wasn't Dad, either.

"Thank you," said Patricia, handing my mother her bag of yarn. "It's good to see you again, Ellen."

"You too, Pat...ricia" my mother replied.

***

We sat down to dinner at the same restaurant where Andrew and I had our first date, though it didn't seem as quaint as it had then.

We were seated between two families, both with young and loud children. One child, who looked about 5 years old, kept being reprimanded by his dad for putting his finger in the flame of the candle. The kid was laughing and snatching his hand quickly out of the flame. His sister sat quietly next to him, just watching.

"I met someone," my mother said before our menus had arrived.

I knew it. "Who?" I asked, trying to not grimace at the thought of my mom dating someone besides my dad. At the same time, I was also trying to ignore the father next to us as he was slapping his son's hand and saying, "No! No!" loudly.

"His name is Bruce," she said. "He's a financial planner."

"Is it serious?" I asked.

"Oh, no, well...no," she said.

"Mom," I said. "I want you to be happy, but this is hard for me. It seems kind of sudden. What about Dad?"

"What about him?" she said, rather coldly. "I waited on him hand and foot for years. He never appreciated it." *Was this the first time I had ever heard my mother say anything negative about my father?*

"Oh, Mom," I said softly.

"You said you want me to be happy. I'm finally happy. Bruce and I have been dating for a few months. We enjoy each other's company."

"Ok," I said, trying to sound indifferent, though I knew I wasn't. "Well, then... that's good."

"Are you dating anyone?" she asked to change the subject.

"Not really," I said unconvincingly.

"Andrew still?"

"Not really, Mom. I haven't seen him lately. I'm not sure what is going on."

"Oh, this looks great," she said pointing at her menu. "I love lamb."

I eagerly took the opportunity to change the subject as well and grabbed my menu with both hands and shoved it close to my face.

Out of the corner of my eye I saw the drama at the next table escalate into an all-out battle. The father finally grabbed the five-year-old, lifted him out of his seat, said "that's it," and took him out of the restaurant. The child screamed the entire way out the door. The mother, still at the table, sat with her head in her hands. The sister stared at her mother.

"Look at her," my mother whispered, motioning to the little girl. "You were like her. You were always such an easy kid. You never acted out. You always did the right thing."

I smiled back at my mom.

"Good things are going to happen to you, Jane."

"Thanks, Mom" I said quietly

"The lobster ravioli sounds wonderful," said my mother, getting back to her menu.

CURSE OF THE BOYFRIEND SWEATER

"Do you want to see pictures of Bruce?" she asked.
No, I don't want to see a picture of Bruce. How could she be dating already?

"Sure."

She took a dog-eared photo from her purse and handed it to me. The picture showed my mother in the summer standing on a dock at what looked like the Jersey Shore with a man holding her. He stood behind her with his arms wrapped around her frame. Her hand was grasping his. He had a beard and a big smile, and held up a glass of white wine. It was one of those photos taken from a pre-digital camera. My mother had red-eye.

"He looks nice," I said. *He looks like a professor.*

"He is nice. I'd love for you to meet him."

I looked at the imprinted date on the photo in the lower right hand corner.

The picture was from two years ago!

I didn't say a word.

"See, don't we look happy?" she asked.

I bit my lip and politely replied, "yes."

Chapter 18: Charity

A lot of knitters hate finishing projects. They hate sewing in the ends of a scarf, crocheting a border on a shawl, or repeating square upon square for a blanket. Rachel, for instance, has left dozens of projects unfinished.

Me? I love finishing projects. I couldn't imagine knitting all the different parts of a sweater and never getting around to seaming. Seeing the parts come together is one of the chief delights of knitting. I guess it's difficult for some people to see the end, but for me, I can't wait to put all the pieces together. It's like finishing a jigsaw puzzle, or like a pitcher getting the last out in a baseball game. It's like finishing a good book. My heart always pounds with excitement minutes before the final stitch.

By the time I was ready to stitch up all the pieces of my blanket, I could barely contain myself. Patricia's pattern was terrific. Each block came out perfectly. The Koigu yarn Patricia had recommended, in solids and multi-colors, looked amazing, and I couldn't wait to see how the pieces fit together.

I shoved my coffee table to the corner of the living room and laid the squares out on the floor. I rotated a square a quarter turn. I switched the left and right squares. I spun the top middle square 180 degrees. I exchanged the bottom-right corner square with the top-left one, and I stepped back to look. The blanket was perfect. I stacked the squares on top of one another so I knew in what order to sew them. I sat on the floor and bent my legs to use them as an architect uses a drafting table. I began sewing the blocks into a blanket.

I sat there, sewing for hours. My hands were tired and my eyes were bloodshot by the time I finished. My sense of accomplishment was only equaled by my exhaustion. The blanket, however, was beautiful!

I turned off the TV and used whatever energy I had left to carry the blanket to bed. I pulled it over me for the first and last time.

I left work early the next day. It was a Friday and a few of my co-workers were heading out early to get dinner. I passed on their invitation since I knew I had to get home and get to the knit shop.

I walked into Patricia's Yarns carrying my blanket in a large shopping bag. On the table, in the middle of the shop, was a hefty pile of newly knitted items. There was a white, cabled wool sweater, two or three baby blankets, and three or more scarves and hats. Patricia, sitting alone at the far end of the table, looked frustrated.

"What's the matter?" I asked.

"Margaux dropped off the damn blanket for the charity auction half-way sewn. She had to go pick up her mother who had a flat tire. So here I am, with two hours to go before the auction, stitching up the blanket and I still have to run home and get changed. *Just once*, I'd like these things to get done early!"

"Where's the fun in that?" I joked. "Here, if it's any consolation, I finished it last night." I held out the bag.

"What's this?" she said, reaching in and pulling the blanket from the bag. "Oh, Jane, your blanket looks amazing!"

"It's not my blanket," I said. "I want the charity to have it."

"Jane, you spent so much time and money on this."

"I know, but it's for a good cause."

"Let me at least reimburse you for the yarn."

"No, but thank you. I loved making it."

Margaux ran into the shop. She was obviously out of breath. Her face was all red. "Is the blanket done yet?"

"No, *Pain in the Ass*, it's not," said Patricia, laughing. "Oh, look, we have two blankets," said Margaux, pointing to my blanket.

"That one is Jane's," said Patricia. "She is donating it to the auction. And guess what? It is FINISHED!"

"I know," said Margaux. "Come on, let me help finish the other one."

"I'll help too," I said.

"Jane, let me get a quick picture of you with your blanket," Patricia asked me while retrieving her Polaroid from behind the counter. "This will look great on the bulletin board."

I posed as best I could, holding up the large blanket awkwardly until I saw a flash. "Looking good," said Trish.

"I promise," Margaux said, pulling out a chair at the table, picking up her blanket, "next year, we'll get this done in September!"

"Right!" said Patricia, rushing back to her blanket squares.

When we finally finished the last stitch, Patricia hung a sign on the shop that said, "Closed for charity auction," and we quickly left to go home and get dressed for the big event.

Teak was an enormous Asian restaurant built in what had once been an old warehouse. The vaulted ceilings loomed high overhead, and on the back wall there was a fish tank large enough to swim in. There were two floors with a long stairway leading upward. From the second floor, the site of the charity auction, you could stand on the balcony and look down on the people having drinks and mingling below. It was a Friday night, so the restaurant was humming. There seemed to be a great turnout for the charity event as well. Hundreds of people were strolling around the second floor. Both upstairs bars already had lines, even though the event was still being set up. The wait staff hefted memorabilia and auction items in and out of the elevator. The auction tables slowly were filling.

Unaware of the elevator, Patricia came panting up the stairs with a large black duffel bag. I saw her speak to a woman at the top of the stairs who pointed at a table in the middle of the room. The table had a placard that read *"Patricia's Yarns."*

The Knitters gathered around as Trish started placing the items on the table. Next to each item, she put a small card that read: "Knit with love by _____, a friend and customer of Patricia's Yarns." My blanket's card had my name on it. A woman came along and placed a small clipboard next to each item so people could write down bids.

The whole group was there: Margaux, Michelle, David, Mia, Chris, Heather, Jamison, P.A., Doctor Doctor, and Anna. My Hoboken friends were usually dressed casually – a jeans and sweater crowd. That evening, everyone dressed beautifully. The girls showed off fancy dresses and the boys donned shirts and ties. I wore my Diane Von Furstenburg, three-inch black heels, and my hair up.

"You look like a movie star," said David, his usually wild and long curly brown hair slicked back into a semblance of tameness. He sported a dark purple shirt, sans tie, and a black pinstriped suit.

"Thanks," I said. "You look very dapper too, my friend!"

"So how's it going so far?" said a voice from behind me. I turned around to see Rachel.

"You made it!" I said and gave her a big hug.

"Do you think I'd miss a chance to come to Jersey?" she joked.

"And you brought someone…" I said.

"Jane, I think you remember Joe…"

"This is 'the guy'?" I said to Rachel with a big smile.

He put out his hand to take mine. "Jane! How are ya? Remember me?"

I couldn't believe it. Apparently "the guy" who Rachel had met was Joe – the real estate agent.

"Of course, Joe!" I said, reaching for his hand. "How are you?"

"Doing good, thanks for askin'." He had an arm around Rachel's shoulders. I didn't realize how tall he was when we first went looking for apartments. He seemed to tower over Rachel. I looked down at his shoes and noticed he was wearing inch-high cowboy boots. "Jane, how's the apartment treating ya?"

"I love it," I said. "I can't believe you two are together. Rachel, why didn't you tell me?"

"Well," she said, "actually it's kind of a new development."

"Oh?"

"Remember the hat you made me?"

"Yes, of course."

"Well, I didn't want to tell you earlier, but I had lost it."
"Oh no."

"I know! I lost it taking the PATH back from here one day. But Joe," she reached over, taking his hand, "found it."

"I did," Joe said. "Right in the middle of the PATH car on my way to Manhattan. I said to myself: that's a nice-looking hat. So I picked it up. I looked at the label: 'This garment was handmade with love for Rachel.' I said to myself: Rachel, knitting. I remember we had talked about knitting while you went looking for apartments. And I don't forget customers in January – not exactly the housing boom kind of time – and I especially don't forget two pretty girls like yourselves."

"So Joe called me," Rachel said, "and asked, 'Rachel, did you lose a hat?' At first I was like, 'Who is this?'"

"I never lose a phone number from a client – it's good business."

"Anyway, I remembered; and, he gave the hat back to me."

I said, "I can't believe you never told me."

"I didn't want you to know I had lost your hat! Besides, no offense Joe, I didn't think I'd like you as much as I do," she said and kissed him on the cheek.

"No offense taken," he replied with a big smile. "And Jane, now that the cat's out of the bag – what do you say to you, me, and Rachel going on down to Mrs. G's for a bowl of Bolognese sometime soon?"

"That sounds amazing!"

"Have you tried it yet?" he asked eagerly.

"No, actually, I haven't."

"What? She hasn't invited you over?"

"I've only seen her a handful of times."

"Then it's gonna happen."

"So, what's the big must-have item tonight?" Rachel asked, smiling, nudging my arm, and looking at the tables.

"There's a certain blanket over there that I hope people like," I said and pointed toward the Patricia's Yarns table.

"Jane," she said, peeking around me, "it's gorgeous."

"You haven't even seen it yet," I replied.

"I can tell from here," she said with a grin.

"Who needs a drink?" asked Chris to the group. Everyone's hand went up. "Oh, let's all get in line," I said.

Throughout the evening I would walk past my blanket. The bidding started at a lowly $50, but by the time I finished a glass of wine, the bidding had reached $250.

"Jane," said Anna, "I just saw someone write on your clipboard."

"Jane," said Margaux, "that woman keeps hovering around your blanket."

"Jane," said Michelle, "some guy just wrote on your clipboard."

"Jane," said Chris, "I think those two are going to fight for it."

Finally, there was an announcement. "Bidding will end on all auction items in twenty minutes. The winning bids will be circled on each clipboard."

"Don't you want to go watch your blanket?" asked Patricia. "Looks like you might set a new Patricia's Yarns record."

"No, thanks," I said. "I'll stay over here." I stood in the far corner with Anna, Michelle, Rachel, and Joe.

After the chairwoman of the Hoboken Homeless Shelter gave a short speech thanking all of the donors, buyers, and attendants, and after servers passed out the final mini-cheesecakes, the party concluded. Everyone was encouraged to stay and have another drink, but bidding had officially ended. Walking to the Patricia's Yarns table, I noticed my blanket had already been taken. Circled on the clipboard were the initials "J.G.M." and the number: $1,000.00.

My blanket sold for a thousand dollars! A thousand dollars!

That night, the knitters were the last ones to leave Teak. We sat at the bar talking, laughing, and joking about what we would knit for the charity next year.

***

"Hey Dad, guess what?" I asked.

"You're getting married," he replied.

"Dad, no!" I exclaimed. "I donated a knitted blanket to a charity auction and guess how much it sold for?"

"50 bucks."

"Dad, no!"

"Hundred bucks."

"I spent more than that on the yarn!"

"Um, two hundred bucks," he said.

"No, it sold for a thousand dollars!" I said impatiently.

"That's great!" he said. "A thousand dollars for a knitted blanket. Wow! That's amazing. I'm sure your mother is proud as well."

"I haven't told her yet," I said.

"You told me first?" he asked, implying I would always call Mom before him.

"Yes, I don't really want to talk to Mom right now," I said.

"I guess you know about Bruce," he said.

"You know about Bruce?"

"Yes, Jane, he was *our* financial planner," he said.

"Aren't you upset?" I asked.

"Yes," he said. "But what good is being upset going to do for me?"

"You could tell her to cut it out."

"Not so easy, Janie."

"...Dad, I love you," I said.

"I love you too."

Chapter 19: A New Beginning

By Thanksgiving, walking anywhere near the Hudson River was out of the question. The winter winds came early, bringing with them cold air and a dusting of snow.

My mother was still dating Bruce and my dad was still alone, but moving on. He was getting together with guys from work more often, and he joined a book club.

Rachel, Joe, and I had an amazing dinner at my landlord's, Mrs. G's. Her Bolognese was as good as Joe had said it would be – maybe better. Joe told me that Mrs. Genovese had been his first grade teacher, and that the two of them have been very close ever since. Mrs. Genovese, spooning a third helping of pasta onto my plate, made it clear that I was always welcome to her apartment, whether she heard the doorbell or not.

***

On a cold fall day, I sat cross-legged in my apartment, a cup of soup on the table and my back to the sofa legs in my favorite knitting position. I was mending a sock that had a small tear down the sole, when I heard my phone ring.

"Hello?" I said.

"Hi, Jane," said a familiar voice.

"Andrew," I said.

"How are you?" he asked.

"I'm good. I'm very good, in fact. How are you?"

"I'm doing well," he said.

"Did you get a new phone?" I asked. "I didn't recognize your number."

"I got a lot of new things," he said.

"What do you mean?"

"What are you doing right now?" he asked.

"Um, why?" I replied.

"Well, if you're not too busy, I'd like to show you something. I'm on Sixth Street."

"In New York?" I asked.

"No, in Hoboken," he responded. "Between Washington and Bloomfield."

"OK. Is everything all right?"

"Yes, everything is great."

"What've you been up to? Where've you been?"

"I'll explain everything. Can you meet me on Sixth?"

"I'm not so sure, Andrew."

"Jane, I know it has been a long time, but I want to see you."

"You haven't called."

"I know. I should have. I'm sorry."

"What do you want?"

"I want to talk to you. I want to see you again. Will you meet me?"

I can't believe this. After all this time. "I'll be there in a little bit," I agreed reluctantly. "What is it?"

"I want to show you something," he said.

I didn't have a clue as to why Andrew was in Hoboken. Curious, I put on my winter coat and headed out the door and walked the three blocks towards Sixth Street.

When I arrived, there was no one there. "Where are you?" I texted.

He walked out of a glass door of a building that said "Morris Advertising."

"What do you think?" he said, holding his arms up, pointing at the four-story brick building.

"I don't understand," I said.

"It's mine."

"Huh?" I said.

I bought it," replied Andrew. "This," he raised his arms again, "is mine."

"Morris Advertising?" I asked.

"Andrew Morris," he responded, placing his hand on his chest. He had a big smile. *He looked good*. He also looked like he had been working all morning. He had jeans on and a t-shirt covered in splattered paint. "Of course, I still have some work to do. The movers are coming next weekend with all of my things. But I'm getting my office set up now. Let me show you."

I didn't know what to say. Andrew took my hand and walked me through the door to his new office. Although the outside was built in the 1800s, the interior was sleek and modern. Three low cubicles took up the majority of space in the front room. An office door with "Andrew Morris" etched on the glass was in the back.

In the front were two chairs - *one with a multi-colored hand-knit blanket draped over the back.*

"It's not going to stay at the office," he said.

I picked up the charity blanket.

"I thought you might want to see it again."

"How do you have my blanket?" I asked.

"How do you think?" he said. "I bought it. Of course, I used my mother's initials. I wanted to talk to you that night, but I didn't know what to say."

"You were there?"

"Yes. But I stayed mostly downstairs."

"Why didn't you just ask me for the blanket?"

"It was for a good cause. Besides, I know you stopped knitting for guys," he said with a smile. "I also didn't know someone else was going to up-bid me to 950 dollars! It's beautiful, Jane."

"Why haven't you called?" I asked.

"I needed to take some time, sort things out."

"What about you and Dennis?" I asked.

"Jane, Dennis was my boss. I hated him. He's an ass," he said.

"Dennis was your *boss*?"

"Yes, Jane. My advertising company was consulting on a joint project with Barnes and Ross. I was on a team that worked under Dennis. He was an obnoxious ass the whole time."

"I thought you were friends."

"No! But with you, him, your history together, I was scared it was getting complicated," he said.

"Then why were you hanging out together?"

"When you work where I worked – you have to take clients out. Obviously, that night didn't go so well. After your friends threw their beers in his face, Dennis practically fired me – by text message."

"That sounds like Dennis."

"Yeah, so, it's ok now. I gave due notice and I was able to finish my part of the project, and leave with enough of a commission to get out."

"That's great."

"It's more than great. It's probably the best thing that could have happened. That, with my savings… I was able to buy this," he said waving his arms and spinning around slowly. "And this!" He said pointing to the blanket.

"So you live here?" I asked.

"Just moved in. My apartment is upstairs."

"Big changes," I said.

"You understand big changes, right?"

"I do."

"I missed you, Jane," he said and walked close to wrap his arms around me.

"I missed you, too."

***

The next day, I strolled into Patricia's Yarns smiling. Jamison, Michelle, Margaux, P.A., and David were sitting around the table, knitting. Five coffees and half of a container of chocolate-covered pretzels sat in front of them. Patricia was working behind the counter. P.A. Jessica was holding her newborn baby. Her little girl was wearing the turquoise sweater I had made her on that sunny day on the pier, way back in the summer.

CURSE OF THE BOYFRIEND SWEATER

"She loves the sweater. It's beautiful!" said P.A.

"Thank you," I said. "I loved making it for her. Baby sweaters are the best – they're so cute and they knit up so quickly."

"What are you going to knit next?" asked P.A.

"I'm not sure yet. I have an idea. I need a new project."

"Thattagirl," said Patricia, walking out from behind the counter. "What are you thinking?"

"I'm thinking I want to make a sweater," I said.

"For you?" asked Patricia.

"No," I said, "…for a guy!" I started piling skeins of a beautiful dark blue-gray, shale-colored yarn on the counter.

"Are you nuts?" said Michelle, clutching her necklace.

"This is so soft," I said smiling, holding a skein up to my cheek. "He'll love it."

"Here she goes again," said Margaux, laughing.

PATRICIA AND ADAM SCRIBNER

David looked like he was about to say something, but decided to stay quiet and just shook his head, trying to focus on his knitting.

Ignoring them, I took the "Men's Sweaters" binder off the shelf and opened it. I flipped through until I came to a traditional V-neck.

"This one is for someone special," I said.

"You know, I think you're crazy," said Patricia, shaking her head.

"Patricia, do you still have the garment labels that you can write on, the ones that go inside a finished project?"

"Yes, they're right here," she said, handing me a basket of them.

"I'll take one of those too," I replied.

Patricia handed me one from behind the counter. It was a small piece of fabric. Imprinted on the label were the words "This garment was handmade with love for _____".

"Are you seriously going to make another boyfriend sweater?" asked Patricia.

"Yep. This is going to be a great sweater," I said smiling.

CURSE OF THE BOYFRIEND SWEATER

"I thought you learned your lesson. The curse is real!" said Michelle.

"Is it?" I asked.

"Yes!" said Margaux.

I took a marker from my purse and wrote on the label... "*Dad.*"

~~BOYFRIEND~~ FATHER'S SWEATER
Written by Margaux Hufnagel

His Sweater

Classic V- neck sweater knit from Fibre Co.'s luxurious Terra yarn.

Finished Bust Measurements
40" (man's small)
Yarn: Fibre Company Terra (40% Baby Alpaca, 40% Merino, 20% Silk) 98 yrds./50g
• 12 skeins in Shale
Needles

- US 7 [4.5 mm]
- US 5 [3.75 mm] and one 16″ circular US5 [3.75mm]

Or size to obtain gauge

Notions

- Stitch markers
- Tapestry needle

Gauge

19 sts and 28 rows = 4″ in Stockinette stitch with larger needle

Abbreviations

k2tog: Knit 2 sts together (1 st decreased).

ssk: (slip, slip, knit) Slip 2 sts, 1 at a time, knitwise to the RH needle; return sts to LH needle in turned position and knit them together through the back loops (1 st decreased).

m1: Using left needle, pick up bar in between sts from front to back, knit into the back loop. (1 st increased)

sm: slip marker

p2tog: purl two together

tbl: through back loop

cont: continue

Stockinette Stitch – st. st. – knit one row, purl one row.

Back

With larger needle, CO 94 sts

Begin 2x2 rib

First row (WS): *P2, k2; rep from * to last two sts, p2.

CURSE OF THE BOYFRIEND SWEATER

Cont to work rib as est until pc meas approx 2" from the beg.

Begin Stockinette
Row 1 (RS): Knit
Row 2 (WS): Purl
Cont in St st until piece measures 17" from beginning ending with a WS row.

Armhole decreases
BO 5 sts at the beginning of next two rows.
Next Row (dec row): K2, k2tog, knit to last 4 stitches, ssk, k2.
Row 2: Purl
Rep dec row every RS row 3 more times and every 4th row one time. (74 sts remain)

Work until armhole measures 8in.

Shape shoulders
BO 7 sts at the beginning of next 4 rows.
BO 6 sts at the beginning of next 2 rows.
Break yarn
Place last 34 sts on holder.

Front
Work as for back through armhole decreases.
When armhole measures 3" begin V-neck.

V-Neck Shaping
Next Row: K37, attach new ball of yarn, K37.
Working fronts at the same time decrease for neck

WS Row: Purl

Next Row RS (dec row): K to last 4 sts on 1st half, ssk, k2. [2nd half] k2, k2tog, k to end.

Row 2: Purl

Repeat dec row EOR 14 times more than every 4th row twice. (20 sts left on each side) ending with a WS row.

Shape shoulders as for back.

Sleeves (Make Two)
With smaller needle, CO 38 sts.

Begin 2x2 rib cuff
First Row (WS): *P2, k2; rep from * to end.
Cont to work rib as est until pc meas approx 2.5" from the beg ending with a WS row.

Change to larger needles.

Next row inc rnd: K2, m1, knit to last 2 sts, m1, k2— (2 sts inc'd) 36 sts.
Row 2 (WS): Purl
Rep inc row every 4th row 5times, then every 6th row 11 times —72 sts.
Cont to work in St st until sleeve meas approx. 17" from the beginning.

Begin sleeve cap shaping
Next row: BO 5 sts at the beg of next two rows —62 sts rem.

Next Row (RS) dec row: K2, k2tog, knit to last 4 sts, ssk, k2 (2 sts dec)
Row 2: purl
Rep dec row every RS row 4 times, every 4th row 2 times.
Go back to dec EOR until there are 32 sts on your needle.
BO 4 sts at beginning of next two rows then BO 5 sts at following two rows.
BO last 14 sts.

V-neck Ribbing
Sew shoulder seams.
Starting at left front, pick up and knit 40 stitches to point of V, place marker, pick up 40 stitches up next side of V, work across 34 back stitches place BOR marker. 114 stitches total.

Rnd 1: k1, p1, to 2 stitches before marker, k2tbl, sm, k2tog rib to end.
Rnd 2: Rib to 2 sts before m, p2tog, sm, p2tog tbl, rib to end.
Repeat last 2 rows until neck back measures 1"

Bind off in ribbing.

Finishing
Sew in sleeve caps.
Using mattress stitch, seam sleeves and side seams.
Weave in loose ends.
Steam- or wet-block to measurements.

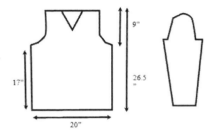

Acknowledgements

Thank you to Tommy Crawford, former student turned editor, knitter, and friend.

Thank you to Harv (Dad), Ruth, Michelle, Jessica, Margaux, and David for all of your help and suggestions.

Thank you to our extremely talented pattern writers, Margaux (a.k.a. Tentenknits.com) and David.

Thank you to our wonderful friends at Patricia's Yarns. You've made our shop everything we always wanted it to be.

Finally, thank you to everyone who reads this book. We hope you enjoy it for what it is – a light-hearted story with a few simple, but favorite patterns.

Knitting Pattern Abbreviations

k = knit
p = purl
st. st. = stockinette stitch
rnd(s) = rounds
m1 = make one stitch
inc = increase
k2 tog = knit two together
ssk = slip slip knit
m = marker
mc = main color
cc = contrasting color
rs = right side
ws = wrong side

About the Authors

Adam & Patricia

Patricia Scribner is the owner of Patricia's Yarns, a yarn shop located in the quaint Hudson riverfront city of Hoboken, NJ. Her husband, Adam, is a Science Professional Development Specialist in the Center for Innovation in Engineering and Science Education located at Stevens Institute of Technology. The couple met in 1995 while attending the University of Rhode Island. Together, they reside in Hoboken with their one year old daughter, Grace, and their dog, Riley. They can be found most weekends at Patricia's Yarns (www.patriciasyarns.com).

PATRICIA AND ADAM SCRIBNER

Project Index

Patricia's Yarns

107 Fourth Street
Hoboken, NJ 07030
201.217.yarn (9276)
patriciasyarns@yahoo.com
www.patriciasyarns.com

Made in the USA
Charleston, SC
19 December 2011